Hervé Guibert, who lives in Paris, is one of France's most gifted writers. For a long time photography critic of *Le Monde*, his fictions include *A l'ami qui ne m'a pas sauvé la vie*, a controversial, moving novel on the last days of Michel Foucault, a close friend, who died of AIDS. This is the first translation of Hervé Guibert in English.

HERVÉ GUIBERT

THE GANGSTERS

translated by Iain White

Library of Congress Catalog Card Number: 91-61196

British Library Cataloguing in Publication Data
Hervé Guibert
    The gangsters
    I. Title
    843 F

ISBN 1-85242-224-6

First published in 1988 as *Les Gangsters* by Les Editions de Minuit,
Paris

This edition first published in 1991 by Serpent's Tail,
4 Blackstock Mews, London N4 and
401 West Broadway # 2
New York, NY 10012

Set in 11½/15pt Bembo
by AKM Associates (UK) Ltd, Southall

Printed by Cox & Wyman Ltd.,
of Reading, Berkshire

for Hans Georg

THE GANGSTERS

'Bonjour madame. We've been asked to spray the trees in your garden. All the trees hereabouts are infested with parasites. Have a look with the lens: that little beastie is what they call a capricorn beetle and it gobbles up everything in its path.'

'You're the workers from the Municipality of Paris?'

'Yes; it's a free service.'

'You'll have to go and speak to my sister – I'm not the boss here.'

Next morning, taking leave of my great-aunts, I find the trees in the garden hacked to bits, the branches piled up in heaps on the bare earth.

*

On Tuesday 14 April I leave for a week in the country on the banks of the Yonne, in the company of T., C. and their children. On the date I should have been in Lisbon with Hans Georg, but the doctor has forbidden it. I have an attack of shingles. Injections of antibiotics, opium-and-belladonna-based sedatives: nothing eases the pains. They recommence and interwine like a diabolically refined flaying. An utterly dull, gnawing cramp threatens my innermost parts with imminent implosion. Most unequivocal of all is a feeling of disembowelment, a single enormous wound that encompasses the entire pelvis, so newly inflicted that the flesh has not had time to grow together. Every movement snarls the stitches. At night, the slightest brushing of the softest of sheets against the skin feels like white-hot steel. Between the disembowelment and the burning, to cap it all, a silkworm rolls its chestnut-prickles, one after the other, over the tormented area. Then, I didn't know that acupuncture, intravenous injections of *eau d'Uriage*, massive doses of vitamin B12 and kaolin poultices could help me. Every evening at mass my great-aunt Louise prays for me. Once, at dinner, my friend Philippe informed me that, scientifically, suffering was such a mystery that one could almost say that it did not exist. T.'s and C.'s children, aged three and one, are instinctively aware of my pain without being told; noisy and affectionately aggressive as they are, this time they enclose me in the glass bell of a quarantine so that I become invisible to their eyes.

*

Contrary to my usual habit I had not left Suzanne the

telephone number of the place where I was going to stay for a week. As a matter of fact I hadn't got it; C. had put off giving it to me and, at the moment of leaving, I had forgotten to ask for it again. It was written on the first floor phone of the house in the country, but what was the dialling-code? What with the children, it was difficult to shout a question from one floor to the other, on top of which an 8 could be a 3 and a smudged 41 had as good as been erased. My great-aunt Suzanne had trouble in understanding numbers over the telephone and found it difficult to handle a pencil and a notebook to take them down; so, for preference, I would phone her, as usual, round seven every other evening, when Louise had gone to mass.

*

Every time I telephone her, Suzanne is allusive, evasive. Usually so animated, she gets unpleasant when I try to draw explanations out of her. All the same, here and there she lets slip odds and ends of curious facts which at first I connect with her bouts of paranoia: 'I don't feel at home any more', 'It's your aunt Louise who's the boss here now', 'I'm afraid she's taking advantage of my helplessness to make somebody the beneficiary of her generosity and her extravagance, but I can't tell you

who . . .' When she succeeds in getting me really
worried, she changes her mind and falls back on
mysterious, rather mocking hints: 'You'll see, you'll
see, no, no, I can't tell you anything more, you'll see for
yourself, oh yes, you'll find things very much changed
when you get back . . .' I don't get flustered: isn't she
just getting her own back on me for leaving? And then,
there's a precedent: a month or two earlier, when I
called one evening to get her news, she announced there
and then, with a tragic air: 'It couldn't be worse. Things
are going from bad to worse. Believe you me, we've
run into a really nasty spot of bother.' I asked her what
it was all about. Her only reply was: 'No, no, I can't talk
about it on the phone, I'll tell you about it on Sunday.'
Was I supposed to wait four days in that state of
uncertainty? I explain to her that one can't worry a
friend like that over the telephone and then let the
matter drop without any explanation. She, who claims
to love me so, replies, before hanging up: 'Oh, but one
can.' Furious, I insist she hand me over to Louise, of
whom I ask: 'But what's it all about?' Louise replies in a
whisper, as if it were a diplomatic secret: 'We suspect
the cleaning-woman of making off with the sheets . . .'

*

The day after Easter the weather clouded over. We take advantage of this to climb the hills to see the cherry trees in bloom. Gipsy caravans are drawn up along the edges of the fields; they are waiting for the flowers to turn into fruit. Each has taken his place in order to keep an eye on his patch of land, held up for about two months until such time as the dusty white will turn into a gleaming granularity; the picking-season is their only official work in the year. Sadly Hans Georg hasn't been able to see the splendour of the cherry-orchards. Caught between the pain of which I constantly complain in a vain attempt to gain relief, the restlessness of the children and the exhaustion of the parents, he left earlier than planned, ill at ease. Shortly before his departure we were in the garden speaking of the rather odd twists and turns into which both our lives seem now to be locked. He tells me: 'We must be under the influence of an unlucky star.'

*

I too returned earlier than planned, the Monday instead of the Wednesday. C.'s brother turned up with his girlfriend and I got them to take me to the station. I had already phoned Vincent to make sure he would be free the evening I returned. I looked forward to seeing him

13

again. The train was packed on account of the Easter weekend. At the worst possible moment a grimy and overdressed old woman seated herself next to me, knocked against my legs with a bag in which she began fumbling for some stinking sandwiches, supporting her bag on my knees. Finally she drew out a duplicated letter, which I did not hesitate to read: it was written by the village priest to his beloved flock on the occasion of the Easter celebrations. It gave the news of the parish. In no time at all I read it – and re-read it to memorise it, so comical the sentences seemed to me: 'The nose of the Madonna has vanished. The all-beautiful has become thoroughly unsightly.' The old woman thrust a hand into her bag and began pawing her rosary. I felt like doing that woman an injury. I recalled Hans Georg's remark: 'We must be under the influence of an unlucky star.' I looked down at the lapel of my dark jacket on which, for a week, a minuscule starfish had been pinned, in the casting of which the tiniest details of the pigmentation had been reproduced. I adored it. Perhaps what I was adoring was my misfortune. Maybe Hans Georg's unlucky star was this starfish; on getting home I unpinned it and replaced it with the angelic little cyclist I'd worn last month, before the starfish. I'd discovered these brooches in December in the toyshop in the Passage Vivienne and I

14

go back there frequently to see if there are any new ones. I've bought dozens, and given them to Mathieu, to Eugène, to T.'s daughter. There's a harp, a sailing-boat with a Lilliputian crew, bears, both Teddy and polar, a fat, satisfied, bristling Angora cat, butterflies; recently this starfish appeared on the little felt board to which they're pinned. I bought it after a moment of hesitation, together with a toad which, out of mischief, I fixed to the flies of a pair of pink underpants which I offered to Vincent. I've found out that it's a young girl who carves these brooches; once she's made a model, she casts a few dozen copies, then destroys the mould so that they become something rare, encouraging col-lectors to exchange them. I'm fascinated by the objects this young girl makes. One day I'll try to make her acquaintance.

*

Back in Paris on Tuesday the 21st at lunchtime, I wait until the afternoon to phone my great-aunts. Usually, after an absence of a few days, I either call in on them or go to dinner with them. On the telephone, Suzanne seems almost put out that I have returned a day earlier than expected. 'Oh! You're back! Already?' she says. 'Oh,' she goes on immediately, 'you can't come to

15

dinner tomorrow, your aunt Louise has to go shopping in Paris. You can only come to lunch on Thursday as arranged.' At seven Vincent rings to cancel our date, so I dine with Philippe. At one point he said to me: 'In any case, you are of course your great-aunt's heir . . .' – 'Not at all,' I told him, 'Louise is the sole heiress. Very often, when Louise isn't there, without my raising the matter myself, Suzanne turns the conversation towards the question of inheritance. "Louise has no idea of the value of money, and with that scatterbrained attitude, she's perfectly likely to end up penniless. She's forever making out large cheques to the Carmelite order and charities like Médecins sans frontières. . . Louise has, to be sure, promised me that your sister and yourself will be the heirs when I die, but with her one can never count on anything. She's so easily taken in, she lets people pull the wool over her eyes. As soon as I die, she'll be fleeced right, left and centre . . ."' – 'It's absolutely essential,' my friend Philippe tells me, 'to have the will changed. It's not a question of disinheriting Louise; what it needs is for her to have the interest the capital earns, and that your sister and yourself have what's called the bare property, the reversion.' I tell Philippe: 'My greatest fear, given my love for Suzanne and the way she's been let down all her life, is that when her time finally comes, given how important my affection is to her, a move of that sort could cause her to doubt it. I'm a fatalist – I'd rather not do anything . . .' It's curious how sometimes, in a roundabout way, one can talk about things before they happen, as if their smell preceded them . . .

*

At five to one on Thursday 23 April I arrive at my great-aunts' house, bearing bunches of tulips and daffodils, along with the tenth-century Japanese courtesan's work *The Pillow-Book of Sei Shonagon*, which I had been reading in the country. As usual, I press three times simultaneously on the two bells of the two apartments. Through the gaps in the wire meshing of the heavy black gate I catch sight of busy presences. The smell of paint and an unexpected agitation. Unknown persons open the gate. I walk into the garden: men everywhere, men wearing blue painter's overalls in the corridors, on the stairs, in the hallway. The weather is splendid. Smart, fresh, yellow and pink paint gleaming on the dilapidated walls. I think: 'So that's the famous mystery, then, another of my aunts' little secrets. Suzanne claimed she didn't want the work done – Louise must have insisted.' The latter hasn't bothered to come downstairs to greet me; she's waiting for me in the corridor on the first floor, warm, unaffected. I remind her I'm not supposed to kiss her; shingles isn't particularly contagious, except with old people with whom it's likely to be fatal. Old men have been known to jump out of windows to escape the pain. Louise tells me to kiss her all the same. I go into Suzanne's apartment: the carpet is rolled up; the cleaning-woman, Sophie, a very cheerful young West Indian I've met once before, has finished her work and is waiting to get her job-slip signed before leaving. Standing next to her, by one of the windows looking out over the garden, I'm not quite sure what to say. Some anodyne, apt remark: 'The paintwork . . .it will liven things up.' And she, with a doubtful or worried grimace, tells me: 'Yes, it's all right . . . perhaps. . .' I come upon Suzanne. One of the first things she says to me: 'We've been wonderfully lucky. There hasn't been a drop of rain in the week they've been here . . .' Instead of her usual delight at seeing me again, I sense only embarrassment, innuendo, coolness. I ask her questions; she's unwilling to answer. She's so strange that I ask myself whether she hasn't gone a bit funny in the head in my absence. All this irritates me. I suspect her of insincerity, of having a bad conscience (six months previously she'd had me start looking around to find somebody reliable who could set about this redecoration work, had called them in, then, impolitely, failed to follow up her enquiry). To every question, she answers: 'I can't tell you anything for the moment, it'll have to wait till the work's finished, that should be tomorrow, then I'll explain everything, but not before.' She says this in such a stubborn, unfriendly manner that I'm inclined to let the matter drop rudely, thereby teaching her a lesson. At the same time I suppose the mood she's in must be the result of the inconvenience caused by the work, and I decide to overplay my annoyance. I tell her: 'You don't deserve these flowers, nor this book.' She replies: 'Oh, the flowers . . . there's nowhere to put them any more . . . they brought us some for Easter, and a chocolate egg. They said we were two old women abandoned by everybody . . .' She puts a lot of emphasis on these words, as if she means them for me. She has no end of nerve. As she leaves, since she's noticed my irritation, the cleaning-woman jokingly remarks: 'Just you see you don't torture her too much.' Time for lunch. One of the workmen, a big fellow, comes civilly to see my aunt and, bending over and speaking in a loud, talking-to-somebody-deaf voice, says: 'I'm going to take advantage of your being upstairs to work here without disturbing you. I've got some putty to put on that window.' – 'By all means, by all means,' my great-aunt says with an expansive gesture. The man exits. I take Suzanne by one hand; with the other she follows the angles of the furniture. Passing her desk I notice that some papers clearly marked 'Income from securities' are scattered, as if they had been disturbed. I say to Suzanne: 'You really ought to be careful.' I cover them with a big envelope, I propel Suzanne before me, hands under her armpits, to help her climb the stairs. At the final step she totters and grasps more nervously at the banister-rail. This is the step that frightens her the most, as if she knew that one day it would be the death of her. I close the door behind us – it had been left open on account of the dreadful stench of insecticide. I notice that the table by the door has vanished. 'They've put it in the front room to treat the wood,' Louise confides in me. 'I needed that table; they told me it was wormeaten, they wanted to burn it, but I want them to restore it.' Suzanne clings even harder to my hand; ordinarily she holds it firmly but gently, in the most trusting of grips. Now I have the feeling she wants to tear it off, that she's trying to hurt me. She manages a half-turn, hauls herself up with all her strength towards my ear, pulling violently at my arm, and tells me, deathly pale and flushed, parched and streaming, in a voice that is both a whisper and a shout: 'All this is being done on the side, they're moonlighting.' I've never seen her like this; she's become a different woman, a madwoman with an oh-so-reasonable air. I burst out laughing, exaggerating my reaction: 'That's not something to make a song and dance about. Not with the neighbours opposite looking on . . .' At table I enquire: 'Are those the workmen who came to see to the parasites in the garden?' – 'Yes, no,' Louise replies with a touch of embarrassment, and, to cut short the discussion, she tells me firmly, with finality: 'They're old friends.' – 'Friends of whom?' I demand. 'Friends,' she answers with a spiteful and definitive air. She has that fixed, slightly crazy gaze I first noticed when, two years ago, the doctor prescribed her over-powerful tranquillisers – she whose innate excitability strangely combines with a remarkable slowness. After coffee, with an hour and a half gone by, I go downstairs again with Suzanne to her apartment. I say goodbye to Louise. I take care to shut the doors and windows in the faces of the men working in the garden and conspicuously watching us. I ask Suzanne: 'You agreed on a price for the work?' – 'Don't speak to me about it,' she replies pathetically, 'I beg you to see it my way, I'll talk to you about it on Sunday when it's all over. I'll be so glad when it's all behind us' – 'Do you remember the estimate you got a year ago?' I say. 'How much did it come to?' – 'Come along,' she says, leading me to her desk, 'and you tell me. I get all confused with these new francs . . .' The estimate for the work is in full view, on top of a heap of papers in a drawer: she's put it aside herself. There are two sheets, clipped together. I can't find any total. Mentally, I add up the figures and reach an approximate total, no matter, at this moment I have a feeling it must be done quickly, I tell her: 'Approximately sixty thousand francs, six million old francs.' She clings to me again, small and fragile, like a teetering vase. She whispers: 'I tell you, we've already paid at least ten times as much.' – 'What are you saying?' – 'Yesterday the boss took Louise in a car to the main post office in the rue du Louvre. I didn't manage to find out how much she paid over to him. She's gone mad. I beg you not to say anything to anybody, to any of our friends. Promise me, won't you?' She flops into an armchair. I say: 'Just stay there and calm down. Everything's going to be all right. I'm going to see Louise. I'll be back down in a few minutes. Don't worry.' I go upstairs to Louise, encounter the workmen again in the corridor, close the open door again behind me, go to shut the kitchen window, say calmly to Louise: 'Sit down. I've got to talk to you for five minutes. How much have you already given to those men?' She replies: 'I don't know. I'm not the boss here, I'm only a servant. Work it out with your aunt. But I tell you, Hervé, if you do anything at all, you'll have lost the confidence I have in you. I'll never confide in you again, because of you I'll leave your aunt, she's helpless, you know she can't live without me, without me she'll die, and you'll be responsible.' – 'It's all one to me whether I lose your confidence or regain it; it's all one to me if you leave Suzanne, she'll find somebody to replace you; but tell me, how much have you given those men?' – 'No, I can't tell you. It would go against my conscience.' I leave her and hurry downstairs to Suzanne's. In the corridor, by the window, a paintbrush in his hand, the big fellow who has been keeping a constant eye on my comings and goings turns aside to let me pass. Smilingly he threatens to dab his brush on my jacket. 'Perhaps you'd like a spot of grey paint on your dark suit?' – 'What a splendid idea,' I say; and I offer him the lapel of my jacket. I notice that his wrists are loaded with new gold bracelets. He glares at the brooch, the angelic young cyclist. If I'd been wearing the starfish, he'd have turned it into a snail. Starfish are fated to be tormented by children in broad daylight. I must not belie my Celtic forename: it means active in combat.

*

Suzanne looks as if a hand has thrust her a bit more deeply into the soft velvet upholstery of the armchair, from which she can no longer extricate herself. She says: 'The foreman has just been here. "You haven't said anything at all to your nephew?" he asked me. "Nothing at all." He left saying: "I'm relying on you."' For the moment I don't know what to do. No doubt about it, I'm afraid; but in the unconsciousness of fear, in its incredible logic, in its coldness, in its calm, I'm dodging the issue. It's only when the danger is past that fear gets the upper hand, sets the heart racing and crushes it, destabilises every fixed position in one's life, and like a tidal wave removes it far from its landmarks. At the apex of danger, fear frees the conscious mind from taking any decision; it takes over the situation. I look out of the window again: nobody about any more. The gangsters have taken my decision for me – they've cut and run. 'They've bolted because you're a man,' Suzanne tells me. Nothing is left, in a sudden silence, but the scattered equipment, blatantly on display like Poe's *Purloined Letter*: the tall metal ladders, the pots of paint, full or empty, the stepladders. At this moment Louise comes on the scene; her ravaged features have a new look about them. The same malevolent reproach at the sight of me, but also the very first indication of deliverance and, visible at last, of fear. She says to me: 'They've gone!' – the implication in her tone being 'It's your fault.' – 'They said, "Something's not quite right, isn't that so?" and I said, "Yes, there's something not quite right, I warned you, it's on account of the last cheque . . ." The big one had only just said, "Your nephew's got such a nice way with him."' I leave my aunts. I imagine one of the gangsters is waiting for me, either in the garage or in the street, to threaten me, or that he's going to follow me; I feel I'm ready to confront the threats and shake off a pursuer. No hand grabs me as I pass the dark door of the garage. I take a quick look into the shed, empty since the departure of the Peugeot: some cartons of invoices, two cane armchairs, the scattered odds and ends left by the gangsters, the chainsaws, the tubs of insecticide, the protective facemasks. A second look, to right and left, into the street, deserted because of the heat. No sign of a passer-by, no double-parked van. I try to imagine seeking help from my friends. I no longer feel able to face up to the situation on my own. Two minutes ago I was calm. Now my heart has started thumping out of control. I think of Philippe: because of his cowboy side, wary, firm and prudent, and because of his official position, he has been able to get himself out of some sticky situations. I take a bus to his office, keep an eye open among the passengers, then the passers-by for a face I might recognise: a tanned individual who got off behind me remains standing at the crossroads, hesitates,

advances, retreats, looks at me, goes three steps down
into the Métro entrance, comes up again, crosses the
road and turns back towards me while I follow him
with my eyes. I ring on the entry phone. I ask for
Philippe. A secretary tells me: 'First floor, right,'
releases the door. I go upstairs. I'm aware that the
secretary will see I'm uneasy. I try to calm down. She
tells me he's out, at a meeting, that he'll be back at
about six. I tell her my name, add that I'll be back
myself at that time, or telephone. I take a taxi. I go to
find T. He has somebody with him. I go into his office,
make my excuses to his visitor, say it's a matter of
absolute necessity, that he must leave us, shut the door
behind him, gaping, flabbergasted. I tell T. the whole
story, tell him I must throw myself on his mercy so as to
relieve this nervous tension a little, so that he can take
matters in hand; for my part, I can barely go on
speaking. He telephones my great-aunts' bank. The
manager in charge of their account is on holiday. He
speaks to the man's stand-in, explains the situation, asks
him to freeze everything until further orders. Then we
take a taxi to the police-station of the *arrondissement*. We
stand aside for an old woman tottering on over-high
heels, clutching a minuscule handbag against her ribs,
wearing an unerringly aligned wig with an unnaturally
pink parting. They guide her into the first cubicle. She

explains how a man doing some work in her place has extorted two thousand francs. The officer treats her almost brusquely, as does the one listening to us, until the moment when, unbelieving, he has us repeat the figures: 'Yes, between six hundred thousand and eight hundred thousand francs.' – 'Old francs, of course.' – 'No, no, new ones!' From that point on, action stations! 'Oh dear, oh dear! But that's a lot of money! That's a serious business, that is! The case will be taken out of our hands by the big boys. They'll have us take statements, then they'll say we've botched it and it'll all have to be done over again. It's not up to me. Yes, but we'll have to listen to monsieur, take down a pre-liminary statement. Go with him right away to his aunts. Get somebody to do it. Who could we send? Whatsisname's on leave. You, what about you? Me, I've got other fish to fry. . . You, don't you fancy going?' While they're beating about the bush, an Asian-looking officer who's listening to my story and taking notes, asks me to describe what type the workers are: 'Arabs?' I tell him I don't know. This isn't hypocrisy; I'm as incapable of recognising racial types as I am of distinguishing ages. The cop gets a bit edgy. I tell him: 'Men with black hair, that's all I can say for certain, between twenty-five and forty, of. . . how can I put it? . . . Mediterranean type.' The policeman explodes: 'But all the same, why didn't you warn us right away?' – 'I was afraid of making a mistake.' – 'We could have made an easy arrest.' – 'Yes, but I'm not James Bond.' The policeman with the yellow, pockmarked skin still doesn't believe his ears. 'Sixty millions! How's it possible?' And then, as a man, as one man to another, as a friend, and as a confidence that all at once draws us together, he says: 'It's true, after all, we're still young, the two of us, but who knows if, when we're that old, we won't let ourselves be ripped off in the same way?'

*

They've assigned us a young inspector in jeans and trainers, a handsome lad, as my aunts would say, and this big, bearded bellyacher who has a score to settle with the other cops. Accompanied by T., we get into the back of a radio-car. It slows up in my aunts' street. I catch sight of Louise, wizened-looking, her black shopping-bag in her hand, returning from a trip to the shops. For her, life is going on as usual. 'We'll have to watch it,' I say to the officers, 'she hasn't been forewarned. She'll be furious.' As the car draws in to the side, I get out to call out to Louise. Before she can close the door, I tell her: 'I've come with T. and the police.' She says: 'Do whatever you like, I'm not the boss here, I'm only the servant, see to it with your aunt, as for me, I've nothing to say.' She slips away. The police check over the completed paintwork, inspect the abandoned equipment. I show them up to Suzanne's apartment. For her too, life goes on as usual; she's reading peacefully, snuggled deep in her armchair, not pretending, really reading, without another thought for the trouble which, two hours previously, had her in its vice-like grip. Seeing us arrive, astonished, she says: 'Well! How did you get in? It's true though, that book you brought me really is a scream. . .' Suzanne is unreservedly ready to answer the policemen's questions. She extracts the accumulated proofs from the pockets of her smock: the statements from the savings-bank, the back of an envelope on which she had begun to add up the sums extorted, a self-styled letterhead on which the foreman had written his name. For a week she's been conducting her own investigation. How did it all happen? 'When they came back after the first weekend, the foreman said: "Since the trees were so badly infected, we'll have to check the interior woodwork, the timberwork and the roof-beams; they'll be worm-eaten: one of these days they'll fall down on your heads." They went up into the loft, checked the bedsteads. When they got to the cupboard door, the foreman said: "There's a crack, just there, we'll seal it

for you, we've got a bit of plaster handy . . ." I asked
him for his identity-papers. He said: "But of course! I
showed them to your sister." I ask my sister, and she
gives me this leaflet with this name written on it, there,
Monsieur Bernard – false of course. Talking among
themselves, they never use their names, and that's why
they never want a cheque – they always say: above all,
no names. At the bank, we drew out the money with
cheques made out to "self" and brought the cash back
here to give it to them. The foreman was very nice. He
would give me a little handshake. At Easter he brought
us flowers and a chocolate egg. He said: "We all
chipped in so the two old ladies shouldn't be too lonely
over the holiday." He had a little moustache and
glasses. I don't know what colour his eyes are, and the
big one has a scar on his cheek, which one I don't know.
The young one was always saying: "I'll carry you,
madame. I'll carry you round in my arms, once the
work's all done, so you can see for yourself how well
my men have worked!" ' Was he reckoning on having
her fall downstairs? Falling with her? An accident.
They call an ambulance, Suzanne is taken to hospital,
her sister must visit her; the coast is clear for stripping
the house bare. We go upstairs to see Louise. As we go
into her apartment. T. is struck by the stench of the
insecticide – very harmful, he tells me – which he finds

exceptionally pungent. Is that how they reckon to do her in? Louise is knitting in her kitchen chair. At first she refuses to say anything. Very slowly she comes out with it, these thoughts that are being taken from her by force. 'Yes, he was a good-looking boy, very white teeth. Never a word out of place, never a coarse word between them, and very nice ways. Despite the capricorn beetles, he spared my blackbird's branch . . . Between ourselves, we called him the gardener. He looked after the garden and the big one did the painting. He told me he trained for four years at Versailles. All those pots of flowers he put in the garden – oh, he really did a good job! Poor dear! Oh, they've had a hard time of it, both of them! The big one's wife died of cancer, suffering terrible agonies, and he, the young one, has a three-year-old son who has a double hare-lip. They don't know whether he'll be able to walk. That keeps him very much occupied; that's why he wasn't here this morning. He took him to a specialist institute near Denfert-Rochereau. You should have seen it, when I got back from the bank and told him the money wasn't there, that the manager couldn't release such a sum in twenty-four hours, he took his head in his hands and moaned, "My child, my child." Then I thought in the meantime I could give him some Treasury bills. I had some in my cupboard. He saw where I took them from but he never took anything. Oh, certainly not, of that I'm sure, I made sure of that, they took nothing away. He was kind enough to come with me to the savings bank on the rue du Louvre. He stayed outside, no, he parked quite a long way from the office, and what's more, when we got back to the car, it was a good five-minutes' walk, he'd got a parking-fine of two hundred and thirty francs. It was about three o'clock. He can't know Paris very well' – or was he pretending not to? – 'he didn't know where the rue du Louvre is, he asked the way five times. The car? Oh, I can't tell you, it must be twenty years since I was last in a car, since we sold the pharmacy. I told him he'd been a decent sort, he took me for a little extra drive, he told Suzanne he'd taken me to the Place de la Concorde, but apparently he didn't know the first thing about it because it was the Eiffel Tower we went to . . . No, the cashiers at the savings bank didn't find it out of the ordinary, I put the bundles in my shopping-bag, we counted them out together, they asked me: "Aren't you afraid to carry all that?" – "No, not at all, why should I be afraid?" There's only two things I'm afraid of, fire and drunken men; I saw some of them in the first war who were terrible, disgusting . . . The foreman didn't want to count the notes again, only the bundles, they trusted us . . .' Then Louise leaves us: she has to go to mass.

*

Louise is a woman in love. Her love affair goes beyond cop stories. At eighty-one, Louise is a virgin. Her flesh has never been in intimate contact with the flesh of any man or any woman, but every evening her mouth sucks the body of Christ. The priest's fingers brush against her tongue. She complains that, nowadays, in church, they give you the host in the palm of your hand. She refuses to touch it. She has to have it directly in her mouth; obstinately she sticks out her tongue at the priest and hides her hands behind her back to make him give in. The priest submits. Louise tells how, during the first war – she was nine – she had been shocked at the sight of drunken soldiers flashing their members from between the half-opened flaps of their greatcoats. Suzanne told me the other day that Louise's sexual education was completely lacking, and that she – for God's sake – didn't feel up to it. The cleaning-woman had just complained that the people in her suburb weren't properly protected, the mayor was an incompetent, girls were being raped, there'd even been a little boy sodomised on a stairway. . . 'Sodomised?' Louise had asked, startled at this new word, 'what does that mean?'

Louise doesn't like being kissed. She's come to tolerate my kisses, but she always wipes her mouth with a cloth, before and after. 'Old people,' Suzanne often tells me, 'are like babies, they need little caresses; but nobody ever gives them any. . .' The foreman, though, he was aware of that. He gave Suzanne little hand-shakes, and he took Louise for a drive; in the sky-blue van, her twenty grand in bundles of five hundred on her knees, Louise saw Paris again for the first time in twenty years. She must have been carried away. Did she let the foreman take her by the hand too? One evening, about three months ago, as she was leaving the church, a young man accosted her and embraced her. Louise told us immediately. But on another occasion, again as she was leaving mass, the young man wanted a repeat performance, Louise forbade him. I ask Louise whether the foreman and the young man aren't perhaps the same person. 'Oh, no!' Louise replies, 'the young man doesn't seem to be quite normal, and he's the son of one of the local tobacconists.'

*

In the meantime the more senior cops have turned up. These are men of another sort, at the same time quicker off the mark and more nonchalant. They don't have to demean themselves to search through things like their local colleagues; their talented eye has immediately discerned the tiny detail that doesn't quite fit, their inquisitive nose is a computer that in an instant distinguishes the clue from its surrounding rubbish. In the garage, the senior police officer inspects the abandoned equipment. He has noticed the amount of paintwork finished in a week. 'I've never seen the like,' he says, passing a finger along a line of grey paint. 'At all events they're not professionals with the brush.' And, in the garage: 'Well, fancy that, what's this we've got here? . . . a box . . . a case, but for what? . . . ah! ah! a watch . . . here's the guarantee . . . oh! anyway, he'll have given a false name and paid in cash . . . April 22nd, he bought it yesterday . . . Yes, they love gold, these Portuguese . . . half of them are Portuguese. The Arab grocer on the corner just told us – they did their shopping there.' (In this context, Louise was astonished that they bought sandwiches for ten francs apiece when it would be cheaper to slip a slice of ham in a loaf of bread.) The officers warn me that the 'dactylo' will be coming in the morning. Nothing is to be touched. Some pots of paint in particular have been put aside in a shed: the 'dactylo' is not the secretary who will be sent to take down a statement but the fingerprint-service. The pleasant young inspector from the local station says: 'Try to calm your aunts down this evening. Don't keep on about this business. Talk about other things to them. We'll be back tomorrow morning between nine and ten to take statements. Your aunts will have to lodge a complaint; that's important.'

*

Suzanne says: 'Louise is mad, she would have let her last sou, her last stitch of clothing, be taken by these gangsters. I already fear the worst. What can we do?' I jump at the opportunity. I make use of it to take up the thread of what Philippe was saying the previous evening: 'It's not a question of disinheriting Louise, you owe her so much, but just of seeing to it she doesn't squander your money on charities or under the pressure of family blackmail. Since you want the money to come to me and my sister, all you have to do is to make over to Louise the interest on your money and to us the capital. The interest will take care of Louise's upkeep; on her death, my sister and I will inherit that as well . . .' At that moment I make an error. It's not entirely myself that's speaking, it's my panic, it's my oh-so-reasonable friends who are always putting me straight: there's no sense whatever in being a fatalist, the thing is to have one's feet firmly planted on the ground! The wily Suzanne sounds me out: 'How to go about it?' she asks. 'It's just a matter of signing a paper. I'll go to a lawyer and make enquiries. Let's do it right away; that'll be safer.' Suzanne gets frightened. 'No,' she says, 'we haven't the time. Louise will be back from mass. She'll catch us at it.' Then I make a psychological blunder. Right in front of Suzanne, I phone Vincent. 'Are you free tomorrow evening?' I ask him. He says he isn't. 'Would you like us to go away for the weekend?' He replies: 'Yes, maybe,' in a tone that means 'this time it's for real.' Suzanne is taken aback at my so openly leaving her in the lurch after my proposal. I want out of the situation.

*

Louise returns from mass. I say: 'So you really did pray for the gangsters? That they'd never be caught?' – 'Exactly,' she replies, 'but I prayed for you as well, as I do every evening . . . Anyhow,' she adds, 'I regret nothing. It's been great fun.' The terror has amused her. I say: 'You'd like to become Our Lady of the Crooks, eh? Before cutting a kid's throat, or an old lady's, they'll cross themselves and whisper your name.'

*

I don't exist. I'm not my great-aunts' little nephew. My reflexes haven't succeeded in checkmating the gangsters. I see the outcome of the story: Louise has become the crooks' accomplice, she helps them torture Suzanne, passes them the tongs, the needles, the burning brands, the cords. With the rag she wipes the blood from the instruments. Mute, stony-faced, she gets her sister to sign away her fortune, their house, then gaily puts her signature to her own destitution, leaves with the gangsters on the pillion-seats of giant motor-bikes, hangs on to their tattooed arms, lets down her white hair so it can fly loose in the wind; and is chucked into a ravine.

*

I'm alone with my great-aunts – dare I say at grips with them? I've decided to stay and sleep at their place. One never knows. Perhaps I'm a bit afraid to be alone in my own place in the evening. According to the police there's no great risk; the gangsters would be unlikely to try to recover their equipment, despite the levers and crowbars they stored in the garage so as to be able to force the door and clear the house out in record time.

On leaving, the young inspector gave me his emergency night-time telephone number, covering the whole district, which guarantees an immediate response.

*

Suzanne's evening meal is soup and stewed fruit; Louise dines on half a bar of milk chocolate and some camembert. I opt to share Suzanne's meal with her; the packet-soup will pass for real soup, and the stewed fruit will pass for tinned. There's the problem of the bed: where am I going to sleep? 'Not with Suzanne,' Louise tells me, 'she needs room to turn over, and besides it wouldn't be proper. No, you'll sleep in the room next to mine. The one your mother slept in,' she adds pointedly. The bed has to be aired. The sheets are still there, they haven't been changed for months, for years. I turn them back and uncover a wriggling maggot. I've turned the light on in my room, and I make sure there isn't any gap between the curtains; I make three attempts at this; I imagine the gangsters could be watching my shadow. After dinner I tell Louise I'm going to have a bath. In that case,' she says, 'we'll have to light the water-heater . . .' She pummels it, bangs it; it's as if it hasn't been used for ages. Some soapy water is stagnating in the bottom of the washbasin: they don't let anything go

39

to waste. The toilet-paper is the wrapping-paper from the bread. Every Christmas I give the old Carmelite luxury cosmetic products – body-shampoos and perfumed oils from Guerlain. I find no trace of these bottles; has she stowed them away in the cupboard? Louise goes off to put Suzanne to bed, then does the washing-up. She's worn out. For months now she's been going round with her eyes half closed. She flits about the gloomy apartment, with the windows open on to the warm night, from one room to the next, turning off the lights behind her as she goes. She doesn't use the time-switch on the steep staircase. What for? She could easily break her spine; her corset would save her, she always says: 'Me? They'd have to beat me on the head with a bludgeon to do me in.' Perhaps the gangsters have understood this.

*

For me the night is a hell, an ultimate trial, an all-powerful suffering insinuating itself into every fibre of my being. Not only do I not sleep a wink, but everything is set up for the night to torment me. Overwhelmed by events, I haven't had the time to buy the kaolin poultices Agathe recommends to ease my pain. My shingles prickles me, burns, itches, has a whale of a time flaring up between my skin and my tee-shirt. I shudder with anguish at the involuntary recollection of the day's events. In Louise's room the interphone crackles impatiently, splutters, blathers, whistles, fizzles; then it stops, like a malicious animal, to allow me to subside into a brief doze – very brief, for it has fallen silent only to recommence all the louder, with my nerves that little bit more on edge, and this time making a noise like chair-legs rattling together, dancing the polka, sneezing, hawking up its lungs (or its batteries) in interminable coughing-bouts. All at once I understand the reason for Louise's half-closed eyes. I even understand how she opened her door to those gangsters, and everything that followed. She's living out a martyrdom. She loves her martyrdom. With that interphone that ruins her nights, her devotion and self-sacrifice are still more admirable: the stairs, climbed and descended, day in, day out, the steps scrubbed, the bottles of water to be lugged about in the black shopping-bag, the waiting in queues at the market, the cooking, Suzanne's clothes, lifting her sixty kilos at arm's length to shift her from a chair . . . 'Your sister is a saint,' Suzanne's neighbours say. I always add: 'Louise, I'll take your body to St Peter's Square to have it canonised.' From now on I have further proofs to add to my case study: the defective interphone is every bit as good as the ravenous

41

lions; the Nazis tried out a similar system – depriving people of their reason and their life simply by depriving them systematically of their sleep. One can die that way, of exhaustion. It's not merely the martyrdom of the interphone, there's the martyrdom of sacrificing oneself for a man with white teeth who has a little lad with a double hare-lip. And the martyrdom is more sublime if one suspects that the man is a crook and a liar, and that one's charity is the subject of ridicule. When I asked Louise if she had prayed for the gangsters, she added to her reply: 'Like little Thérèse, who prayed, you know . . .' – 'Yes,' I said, 'for Pranzini, the criminal condemned to death, it's well known . . .' – 'Well, faced with the executioner,' Louise told me, 'Pranzini was converted to God . . .' Is that not the most sublime of torments to inflict on oneself: to betray a trust and, on an impulse, under threat, to abandon one's old and infirm sister, caring for whom one has sacrificed one's life for forty years?

*

Six months previously, one night, wanting to get out of bed for a pee, Suzanne slips, loses her balance, and finds herself hanging over the edge of the mattress. Clinging on with all her strength, she pictures herself on the floor, her bones broken. She shouts. Louise doesn't respond. For hours she hangs on and calls out. When, next morning, in a distressed state, she tells me what happened, I take matters in hand. The simplest solution would be to have Louise sleep with Suzanne, but Suzanne, the boss, likes her comfort, and for Louise, the servant, carnal promiscuity isn't conducive to prayer. Something else must be thought of. My doctor says: 'A female urinal.' T. says: 'An interphone that plugs into the mains.' I run about Paris to buy a urinal, then an interphone. Suzanne won't have the urinal. She says she can't spread her legs properly because of the osteo-arthritis in her hip; she's repelled by all the visible signs of senility. I explain to her the workings of the interphone; the whole business is a shambles. A few days later Suzanne tells me, with a mysterious air: 'They're trying to get in touch with me' – 'Who? Your late husband?' – 'No. People, though; there's no doubt about it. They've bought interphones too, so's to communicate with me in the night.' – 'You think it's a network of swingers?' She's annoyed at my making fun of her. 'There's nothing more I can tell you.' That's how she closes the discussion, with an air of the utmost secrecy. Since, time and again, Louise complains about the nocturnal racket, I end up taking the interphones back to the shopkeeper. He plugs them into the mains, reverses them. Not the faintest crackling. I stick to my guns, tell him what my aunts have told me. Suddenly he hits on the solution; it's because we haven't connected the two plugs in the same direction. 'Look, there are two poles, the negative and the positive; all you have to do is to connect the two plugs in the same way and you won't hear anything any more.' I return in triumph with the interphones, reconnect them correctly, explain to my aunts how they must do it. We wait a bit. The devices don't make any more noise. My aunts seems to have understood; my only anxiety is that, since they disconnect the extensions every morning for fear of wasting electricity, they may reconnect them incorrectly in the evening. That night, harassed by the interphone's hellish tricks, I suspect that Louise is deliberately connecting it the wrong way round – the better to suffer, to live out her martyrdom to its furthest limit. Is it not divine to inflame the wound of destiny with a few drops of boiling pitch? I am submerged, that nightmarish night, by a terrifying feeling of pity. Have I, until now, experienced it to this degree? No, never. It's something horrible: it's exactly that; these are the only words I can use to explain it – I'm doing them justice and delivering them from their reputation as clichés – poignant, heartbreaking.

*

I go over it all again in my mind; the two old, impoverished women, left to their own devices, terrorised for a week by eight gangsters, have felt senility taking them by storm. In a matter of a few months everything has slowly been transformed. It began, it would seem, with a rat which had run across the garden, then got upstairs, taunted Louise by darting between her legs, turned up its nose at poisoned pellets, went downstairs into Suzanne's apartment, took up its quarters in her holey mattress, and gave away its presence by nibbling at her Sunday croissant. From now on, to preserve it from the rodent's greed, the croissant is suspended in one of the windows in a plastic bag, a transparent bag, perhaps to remind her there's a croissant there and it must be eaten, not out of hunger or because she fancies it (Suzanne tells me she hasn't either the appetite or the inclination) but so that the ritually purchased stodge shouldn't go stale. Suzanne is terribly afraid of lapses of memory. Her – infrequent – comings and goings about the apartment are now signposted with little twists of paper torn from used envelopes, scattered here and there, on which she has written the unlikely words that have escaped her in a forgetful moment and which she has spent days and sleepless nights in retrieving. Thus there are aides-memoire: 'honeysuckle', 'Arachon', 'heliotrope', 'Chaliapin'. These useless, unusable words, obsessively repeated, wind up creating a stage, a frame, a crazy image which takes the place of real life; gradually, against a background of mental collapse whose culmination is constantly held in check by medication, the key to the whole of life shows every likelihood of being summed up in this formula: Chaliapin, in Arachon, sniffs at a bouquet of heliotrope in a honeysuckle-thicket.

*

I get up, washed-out, at ten past eight. I put on the clothes into which, the day before, I sweated like a pig. Louise hands me a saucepan of cold coffee which I reheat. I'm shivering with cold. I bite into an over-salty biscuit and spit it out again. Suzanne has slept like a baby and is as fit as a fiddle; she's resolutely awaiting the visit from the police. About half-past nine I go downstairs to open the door to them. First to arrive are the two inspectors from the local station, the pleasant young one, typewriter in hand, and an older superior who has not previously been here, the one who, yesterday, at the station, said: 'They'll have sucked them dry.' He's the one who is to take my statement, in writing, while the young one, smiling, patient, speaking loudly and distinctly, questions Suzanne. In my replies, which I dictate to the inspector, I do my best to be concise and pack in the maximum of facts, with a precision in the wording that prevents misrepresentation. The officer goes over them, tries to rework them into the jargon of a statement. In the process clear, plain words become deceptive and vague. I politely stick to my way of putting it. The inspector gets edgy; from time to time, as he takes his notes, he explodes, he grinds out from between clenched teeth: 'Ah, the shits! The shits! Attacking old ladies like that! It's like attacking children! That lot, I'd cut their heads off, no messing!' – 'Isn't that a bit over the top?' I suggest discreetly to him. 'There hasn't been any physical violence . . . just moral violence . . .' That really gets him going. 'And you tell me that, with what I've seen! Only moral violence! As if that wasn't anything! Me, I've seen poor old ladies go off their heads, monsieur, with schemes like that, and you know what that means, don't you, going off your head? Ah, the shits! Believe me, if I get hold of them, they're going to get a good doing over! I caught one, not long ago, a gipsy he was, who'd attacked an old lady; he was a pretty sight when he left the station!' The surprising thing is that this man of the guillotine is a nice guy. He finishes taking my statement, doesn't let it drag on too long, three sinewy pages of it; there's not got to be any flim-flam. Just before he gets me to sign it, Louise comes by, shopping-bag in hand. 'I'm just off to do the shopping,' she says. 'Ah, but no, madame; I'm going to need your help, now that I've done with monsieur.' I say to Louise: 'I can do the shopping for you; what do you need?' – 'Milk, two long loaves, on the soft side, cut in half, and the paper – that'll keep your aunt amused.' The officer suddenly looks up from his paperwork. 'What do you read in the way of a paper?' The reply reassures him: '*Le Figaro*.' – 'That's a very good paper,' he declares solemnly. 'You know what I read it for,' Louise says, 'the births and deaths . . .' The man of the right – and proud of it – changes the tack of his outrage; he says to Louise: 'Swine like that, they ought to be given an injection and put down, like dogs.' Don't talk about dogs to Louise, especially the injections that put an end to their days. That gets her back up, she protests: 'Oh no, monsieur, dogs, I've had three of them put down. I've seen their eyes when they have the injection; if you'd seen that, monsieur, you'd never dare say that . . .' Suzanne, for her part, isn't in the best of shape. The interrogation has been slow-paced and pleasant to be sure, but it has tired her out. Now that it is over, she is beginning to realise what has happened to them. She asks for something for her heart. Louise gives her a pill which she crushes with a pair of nutcrackers. She explains the procedure to the young policeman: 'When one no longer has one's own teeth, and one's dentures are useless, this is a very useful little trick . . .' The men from the 'dactylo' section have arrived for the prints: little goatee beards, spectacles, bags tucked under their arms, they look like walk-ons called in to play the role of the poor sickly wretches in the stalls of dubious cinemas, anonymous figures who emerge one day from their obscurity to admit in a newspaper that this appearance had behind it its own idiosyncrasies. Unfortunately the prints on the beer-cans, all smeared with paint, are not clear. I ask whether there isn't perhaps something to get from the cardboard wrappings of the Easter-egg they brought. 'No. It needs a smooth surface. Glass, that'd be perfect.' I come back with the shopping: Louise notices, with an undisguised dejection, that the milk isn't the kind to which she's accustomed, and no doubt it's more expensive too; I tried two bakeries for the long loaves, a bit on the soft side, but I slipped up about the milk. I let her get on with it. I've had my fill of this business, of these women, of their fecklessness, of their lack of gratitude. The cops will be back in the afternoon at about three and they'll be sending a team to take away the equipment, so that the gangsters won't be tempted to do it themselves. In the street – or in the way I look at the street – once again, but in a different way, everything has changed: the perspectives are no longer the same, my antennae have gone on the blink, they're no longer sifting things in the same way, the world is no longer divided into people who are attractive or those who are invisible. No, what strikes me is that it is filled only with the guilty and their victims. It's frightening how the look of people's faces increases the number of potential murderers. 'You know,' I say to myself for the first time in my life, 'it's true; there's no end of foreigners in Paris . . .'

*

I snap out of it: shave, wash my hair, stop myself falling asleep and go out again. There are lots of little sky-blue vans parked in my street. I notice, *a fortiori*, that the street is overrun with Portuguese: my caretakers are Portuguese, the caretakers next door too, and the hairdressers downstairs where I live, and the people who run the restaurant just down the road; am I maybe involved with a mafia that watches all my comings and goings, intercepts my mail, and has had me followed for months in order to pull off this scam? On the rue de Rennes, without really thinking about it, I find myself drawn to the shop-windows with dark glasses in them; they're the only things that now attract me. What I finally buy are new interphones, to save Louise from her martyrdom, to deprive her of it by force. Arriving at three, I say to her: 'I'm giving you these to reward you for your generosity to the gangsters ... Everything I've been doing for you since yesterday is only out of pity.' And I launch into a tirade against suffering; I don't know what's got into me. I'm the first to be surprised at the violence of this diatribe I deliver for Louise's benefit: 'Suffering is the most obscene thing there is. I know that, now that I've been suffering for a month. It's filthy, repulsive, and I hold it against Christianity for giving you a taste for it ...' Suzanne is lying on her bed doing a crossword. She invites me to lie down beside her to rest while waiting for the police. It's not the first time she's had this idea: on various pretexts, to listen to music with her on Sunday afternoons. I've always refused. I know this was also my mother's dearest wish: 'To lie down beside me.' This time it's I who am dreaming of that place on that bed, of losing myself there. The infernal Louise, whose snooze I've interrupted, is dead keen to wear herself out: all that shambles they've left behind, it won't please the neighbours; let's slog away, scrub, tidy, tear our knees to shreds crawling about on all fours. Let's lug weights around and give ourselves stunning hernias, let's work ourselves divinely to death . . .

Alone with Suzanne, I remember and home in on a stray thought that had occurred to me a few hours earlier: 'They brought you flowers . . . That reminds me of the young girl who was to have worked here before the cleaning woman; she brought you flowers too. Portuguese, wasn't she? . . . That was how long ago?' – 'Before the winter,' Suzanne replies. 'How many times did she come?' – 'About ten.' – 'She did the housework ten times?' – 'No, only once. But she often called in for a chat. She was a sweetie. No, it couldn't be her.' – 'What was she called?' Suzanne tries to remember, fails. 'You're so cautious. I'm sure you must have written her name down somewhere . . .' – 'Just a moment, yes, perhaps . . . Go and look on my desk, in the place where you found the cleaner's details for the police . . . Under that paper there ought to be a notebook. If I wrote down her name, it'll be there.' I finally find the notebook. Under my aunt's questioning the young girl has written down her name, her address, her telephone number, the names of her employers, the date of her entry into France, her immigration-card number, her social-security number. 'How could you be so suspicious?' Suzanne asks me. – 'You live here together for forty years, you've never had any problem, and now, within a year, you have two cleaners, one after another . . .' – 'No, three,' Suzanne tells me, 'because one day they sent us a replacement for Sophie, not because she was on holiday, but because her son was ill. She only came twice. We didn't like her. We didn't want her back. She read the letters over my shoulder when I opened them; she used to say: "Ah, that's your pension!" "Ah, that's the rent from your tenants!" A thirty-year-old blonde. We never knew her name. And your aunt Louise said: "It's funny, she says she hasn't got a penny, and yet she takes off for a month on the Riviera."'

*

When I confide this lead about the cleaners to the superintendent he notes it down, grumbling. He regards me as a nuisance. He looks as if he's thinking: 'You're not going to teach me my job, sonny; for starters, how is it you want to shunt us off on to those poor women – couldn't be, could it, you've got something to hide yourself?' He says: 'Anyway, we'll listen to everybody, we'll listen to you again too, and we'll listen to your sister. You don't ever see your sister? You don't like your sister, do you, eh?' I burst out laughing. 'That's not the problem; it's just that she lives in Estampes and I in

Paris, and that's not so near . . .' He has a sidekick with him. Again and again he telephones for the van to come and clear away the equipment. Finally they tell him he'll have to lend a hand with the removal. He explodes: 'That's not my job! I'm not dressed for that! I'll be sending them my laundry-bills!' When I bid him farewell, I realise that, as far as he's concerned, as far as they're concerned, I'm the prime suspect. An open-and-shut case: the nephew, impatient for his inheritance, who gets his pals to do the job.

*

Behind the window of a passing bus, I see a young boy who attracts me. What is it, though, this everyday gaze, this gaze that's so haunting? What is it that gives it its power? Might it not be precisely the thing I've just been denigrating, loud and clear – suffering? That thing which doesn't exist. That mystery.

*

As soon as I get back to my own place, I take a spraycan of a blue cleaner for the windows; I set about getting rid of the traces of white powder on the penknife, on the mirror, on the frames of the photos hanging in my room. These minute traces have been there for months. I've left them there deliberately. I have the feeling that only I can recognise them; at certain times of day, and when the light falls at certain angles, they evoke fond memories of evenings spent with Vincent.

*

I think: I'll deny it, I'll say no. Supposing they put the question. Michel wasn't the sort to say: 'You must do this or do that,' his precepts were vague, frivolous. For all that, twice in the course of our seven-year friendship, he repeated gravely: 'If, one day, the police ask you if you're homosexual, you must say no. It's no business of theirs. It's an invasion of privacy. Next thing, they'll use it against you . . .' At the time he seemed to me paranoiac and a bit out of date. Now I'm inclined to take my dead friend's only piece of advice. No, certainly not, not at all. My books? Oh, come now, what have those nonsenses got to do with reality?

*

About a quarter past seven I telephone Suzanne. She says: 'I'm exhausted! It's not just those policemen going on and on that's tired me out; I'm beginning to

understand why there are so many thieves and why they
are never caught. With such a bone idle lot for
policemen, it doesn't surprise me that they live the life
of Riley! You should have seen how they shifted the
equipment out – they didn't fancy dirtying their hands!
I promise you the gangsters would have put a bit more
go into it!' At about seven-thirty, I get through to
Vincent. I explain what's happened. I cancel our
weekend. I tell him: 'I have to stay with my aunts to
give them moral support.'

*

Philippe takes me to dine on a terrasse in Saint-
Germain-en-Laye. He asks me to tell him what's
happened. He says the young Portuguese woman who
brought flowers but didn't do the housework is a good
lead. He urges me to go next day to slip a word about
her to the young local inspector, seeing that it concerns
his district. At a certain point, Philippe says: 'As far as
old people are concerned, there's no contrast in things.
Everything is flat.' New francs and old francs, riches or
poverty, generosity or meanness, the good or the
wicked, the truth or lies: where, after all, is the
difference? Often, lately, Suzanne has looked at me
with a strange fixity. When I've asked her why, she's

replied: 'My sight is going, so I'm photographing you.'
She often sees only half of my face, she says, the part the
light catches; not the slightest feature of the part in the
shadow stands out; the second part of my face is only a
dark blur. Everything dark no longer has any contrast,
has gently faded into invisibility. The night, for
example. At night Suzanne can no longer make out
anything at all, to such an extent as to call out to Louise,
whom she sees going back and forth in front of her
when, in fact, she's in bed upstairs.

*

I start working on this narrative on the morning of the
25th April. It's amazing how quickly the writing goes,
like an arrow in the inanity of time.

*

Every Saturday I lunch with Claire. I'm a bit early. I
take a stroll in the gardens of the Palais-Royal. The
weather is fine. I go up to a bench. Somebody has put a
notice on it forbidding people to sit there today
between one and five. I look at my watch; we're
already within the forbidden period; there's a death's-
head on the piece of paper, but two young Japanese girls

57

have already tossed it away and are sitting quietly on the bench, where, in my turn, I take my place. Suddenly I ask myself whether I haven't already seen the big fellow: about two months ago, in the Algerian restaurant on the rue d'Alésia, I noticed a man like that, fat as a belly-dancer who hasn't jiggled her belly enough, all decked out with glittering gold, with an odd look about him, half way between the effeminate and the ex-convict. That evening I was ill-at-ease. I'd gone to meet The Poet – that's what we'd nicknamed a young friend – at the station. All the restaurants I'd wanted to take him to were closed. It was raining, and The Poet was asking me irritating questions: wasn't I afraid of being short of money in my old age, how much did I earn in a month, etc. Stupidly, I allowed myself to tell him how much tax I'd have to pay in the next year, on account of exceptional circumstances (two successive redundancies with their golden handshakes). I'd earned a fair amount of money in the last year. I myself was impressed at the amount. It was stupid to whisper it so nobody would hear; seeing my embarrassment, The Poet made me repeat the figure. Leaving the restaurant, with all eyes fixed on us, I told myself I'd been less than careful. If the big man had been the person at the next table, had he perhaps, impressed by the figure, had me followed?

*

After my lunch, I took the bus to go to see the young
inspector who'd fixed up an appointment with me at
the local station, and to tell him my leads. An elegant
old man, wearing a hat and a cravat, sat down opposite
me, set a wrapped pot-plant on his knees, and began
gazing fixedly at my angelic young cyclist. After five
minutes, excusing himself, he asked me the meaning of
this badge. Then I asked him about his own: two little
parallel woven lines, red and yellow, across his button-
hole. He said, without arrogance, that it was the highest
military decoration of the 1914 war, that it was thanks
to him I was a free man. Instead of thinking: 'you're a
pain in the arse, you old fart, with your antediluvian
bullshit,' I congratulated him on his valour. He told me,
again very pleasantly, without showing off, that he was
ninety. I asked him how he kept so fit. 'I get up at seven,
I go to bed at ten, have a good meal at midday with half
a bottle of good Bordeaux, but I don't drink in the
evening and eat only something very light, soup, an egg,
a fruit; apart from that, I drink a litre of water a day,
and I take exercise . . .' I told him my routine was pretty
much the same as his; he told me off: 'You're far too
young to go to bed at ten. There's pleasures to be had –
the cinema, the theatre, television . . .' He watched

television, but not everything, he liked films that confirmed and reinforced his perceptions, and the documentaries. He didn't care for the love-stories, because, he said, smilingly and without vulgarity: 'I have my own love-stories, I don't need other people's.' I said: 'You have happy memories?' He replied: 'Yes, monsieur, I have excellent memories; I was sixty-five years with my wife.' Then, with the good taste of not showing any sadness, but with, as it were, a great surprise: 'She's just died.' We alighted at the same stop; I told myself, with irony, one could easily take such a dear old grand-daddy to the cleaners . . .

*

I was taking the piss out of myself: Louise had been in love with the man with the white teeth – and wasn't I falling in love with the nice young inspector in jeans and trainers? As soon as I set eyes on him again, this possibility vanished: he'd cast aside everything about him that was attractive. He was nothing but an employee of the police, irritated by my obstinacy, almost unpleasant. The case no longer interested him, it was no longer any concern of his; the higher-ups had taken it out of his hands. His expression was as inscrutable as that of a nobbled witness. I told him: 'It's like a tangled skein one slowly draws out in one's memory. Every now and then there are flecks of mica caught on the thread that flicker . . .' Sitting opposite me, the young inspector from the local station had become amnesiac: what I was saying was all Greek to him.

*

In the evening, at T.'s place, prompted by C., I once again told my story. At every telling, it further coalesces into a narrative formed, or perhaps deformed, by writing. I haven't admitted to T. the outset of this work, which dates from this morning. My work is the principal distance between us; it has its origin in language, when it becomes the reflection or the accompaniment of writing. I no longer speak as T. does but as one who is working on his story and who, from one day to another, sacrifices everything to it, his thoughts, his sleep, his conversations, as to an imperious, exhausting lover. This evening T. is sardonic, almost aggressive: he's having problems with his work; when this happens to him, he never talks about it, he turns in on himself to deal with his block. If by chance, unforewarned, one lets drop even the most trivial of snide remarks in the course of one of these frantic periods, he wilts, he caves in. When I catch him in that state I'm like a sponge that doesn't understand why it soaks up water. By an immediate transfusion I've tapped into his misfortune; it's within me, but impossible to analyse; I become T.'s armour, pierced with a thousand treacherous holes. I tell C. about the way the big gangster glared at the angelic little cyclist. T. has sensed the fast one I'm pulling in the story. He's snide; he says: 'As always, you bring everything back to yourself.' C. comes to my defence, tells him he's not wanted. T. goes off to bed half-way through the meal. C. goes up to see him and says he won't be coming down again. Before calling a taxi, I in turn go upstairs to see T. He's lying in the dark in his room. I speak his name. He sits up. I sit down on the bed, take him in my arms tell him I love him very much, that he mustn't lose heart, that everything gets better after it has gone very badly.

*

On the 26th of April, at Sunday lunch, my aunts reproach me: not only has the painting work cost them close on sixty million, but, on account of my cussedness, the staircase still has to be done. Am I going to have to take up the brush to satisfy them? 'The two foremen must know you, they must have a pretty good idea of your psychology. They've homed straight in, the two of them, on your little weaknesses. The two of them have worked you over in their minds, body and soul. You, Suzanne, your avarice: it makes me sick to hand over 15 per cent to the state in value-added tax. They're already robbing me blind with their income taxes; like the thief that's been robbed, you're going to pay ten times over; on that basis the blackmail can get under way: "We're costing you plenty, but you run the risk of paying a lot more if you talk. All this work is being done on the side, moonlighting, and you've accepted the principle. You'll have to pay a whopping fine, and that'll leave you penniless." You, Louise, with your Christian charity: "My little son has a double hare-lip. If I don't give a lot of money to the doctors to save him, it's not even certain he'll be able to walk . . ." Perhaps they were well informed about me too, coming on the scene the very day I was supposed to leave for Lisbon: I had my shingles, then finally left for the country . . . The foreman, the man with the white teeth, glasses and the little (no doubt retractable) moustache took good care, the day I turned up, never to pass me in his comings and goings between the garden, the stairs and the second and third floor. I never even saw him.' All this no longer interests my great-aunts. The only thing that matters is the amount of money that has been extorted from them. 'I'm almost certain we'll never lay hands on it again,' says Suzanne, 'and it's the money I intended for Louise, for her old age.' Louise, for her part is cheerfully reconciled to her loss; '*Inshallah!*' she says. 'As long as we can drink champagne' – as on every Sunday, she has just opened a bottle of fizzy wine bought at a supermarket for 92.70 francs – 'and when we can't drink it any more, oh well, we'll have to drink rotgut . . .'

*

This Sunday evening I'm in a bad state. I've slept in the afternoon. I'm alone, and this isn't the right moment. I call Vincent. His father answers: 'All I know is that he's gone off with his crash-helmet.' As long as I've known him, Vincent has dreamed of having a motorbike. He told me: 'We'll go off together on my motorbike when I have one.' Every time, I think 'that would be a fine way to die . . .' Philippe isn't free tonight, Mathieu isn't back yet from Brazil. After yesterday evening, I don't feel inclined to go back to T. and C.'s place. I won't be having dinner tonight, my aunts stuffed me full of oxtail at lunch. Contrary to all expectation, the telephone never stops ringing, but without distracting me from this painful sensation of solitude. It's people I never think about, who never call, and who appear to be in cahoots. I'd rather stay on my own. I open a bottle of Sauternes, begin smoking one of the cigars the actress S.A. left me, then immediately stub it out feeling sick.

The story of Hamsun's book *Mysteries*, which I was reading enthusiastically, no longer appeals to me; it's as if it were competing with my own. As a result of the wine, melancholy becomes torpor. I again consider suicide; this evening I would have to bang a hole in the wall with my head. Suddenly, without premeditation, I go to my desk, pick up the paper-knife and unhesitatingly open the little yellow letter Pierre sent to Vincent at my address. If anybody had said to me, half an hour ago, 'You're going to open that letter,' I'd have said, 'That's a shamful thing, and I'd never do it.' Now that the letter is open, it seems such a human thing to have done! Pierre's little note is a nice one. He posted it in Florida. It's a lover's letter, and he was a bit naughty to make me his go-between, since, as regards Vincent, there is the beginning of a rivalry between us. I found a yellow card with 'Boat House' printed on it; underneath he'd written: 'I'm just where I'd like you to be. I like it a lot, but you'd adore it.' I immediately put the card with its torn envelope in a white envelope addressed to Vincent with this note: 'I kept this sealed letter for you for a fortnight. Will you forgive me for being so lacking in tact this evening, and for having opened it?' How did it come about that I never sent the double letter?

*

On the night of the 26th and 27th workmen put up enormous posters in Paris announcing the candidacy of Le Pen as President of the Republic. They show his ugly mug emerging from a turbulent crowd; the slogan: 'Frenchmen to the Elysée.' These posters, which I come upon when I leave my place on Monday morning, fill me with a violent disgust.

*

On the 16th of March 1986 (I find this date on the first rubber stamp on my first elector's card), I vote. For the first time in her life, Suzanne doesn't go to the polls; she's giving up her right-wing vote. Jokingly, I tell her she can confide in me and make me her proxy. Louise, for her part, is milking it for all its worth. I question her, in passing, during lunch: 'Oh no, I don't like Chirac either,' she says. 'Barre?' – 'No, he's changed a lot.' – 'Who are you going to vote for, then?' – 'For Le Pen,' Louise replies placidly, 'he's the frankest.' I try everything to dissuade her, I even go so far as to filch her elector's card. She's obstinate, and for her it's an inward struggle: she's aware that what seems natural to her distresses me deeply, she's very fond of me, she doesn't want to depress me, but at the same time she's honest and doesn't want to turn from her convictions. Just before she leaves to vote, I deliver my last admonition. I think: now I'll let it drop: I won't even ask her what she finally did. When she returns, Louise seems all tensed up with her struggle. She insists on my listening to her telling me that she did indeed vote for Le Pen, that she doesn't want to lie to me. She's trying to wind me up. So I say to this eighty-one-year-old virgin: 'It's true it's no business of mine, any more than it's any business of yours that I suck cocks. It's the same obscenity, you as far as I'm concerned, I as far as you're concerned, the same strangeness, the same exoticism . . .'

*

All night this lack of cock has tormented me. To remedy the situation, in the restlessness of my insomnia, I've masturbated twice. I've snorted amyl nitrate to give substance to the illusion that I can sniff, lick, then swallow the enormous cock, crudely sketched on the page of a porno-mag, of the young god Pan sprawled naked on a tree-trunk, that it really is in my mouth – the momentary relief of the image. I can feel the various tranquillisers they've prescribed for me, day after day, for my shingles, ascending slowly towards my suffering, but in their ascent they're becoming breathless and lose their foothold. They've cut off the feet of my suffering, but what's the use of that since they're leaving me alone with its head, with its paroxysm?

*

I've suggested to T. that we lunch together, that I call in for him at the agency. I have the feeling that, as far as Vincent is concerned, we've been going a bit too far; for years on end I've myself been so jealous of T.; now I'm astonished to see that, in my turn, I've succeeded in making him furious by talking to him about Vincent . . . T. , for his part, has begun to have need, in increasing, immunising doses, of the pain I inflict on him by my stories. I've been cagey about things; he's been wanting to know about them, so as to be able to jeer at them. Because this relationship with Vincent is to him unimaginable, and thus unshareable, this is what most leaves him out. I tell T. that these games have wound up spoiling our erotic friendship. For a month now we haven't been to bed together. At my suggestion, we decide not to speak about Vincent any more.

*

In the afternoon I make a kaolin poultice and curl up in bed, wrapped in a towel; I doze, lulled by the prickling of the clay, the leech of pain. The telephone rings. It's Louise. She speaks jerkily, without stopping for breath: 'The foreman has called. He said: "Your nephew is sticking his neck out. We're dealing with him since that's what he seems to want. In the meanwhile we'll be coming to see you."' Louise's response was impeccable: 'That's impossible. In any case I won't be opening the door to you. The police have come. They've asked us to lodge a complaint, and we've done so.' The gangster hung up. A threat which from second to second weighs on one, which turns the world upside-down; it's a tide that breaks down the body's sea-walls; an anarchic rhythm invades it. It is not only the heart that beats out of all control, the mouth goes dry. Fear triumphs. 'Cheer up,' Louise says; and, before hanging up, she adds, seemingly more concerned with this problem than with death-threats: 'Your aunt Giselle's spending next week here; tell me, would it bother you if she slept in your sheets?' I reply ill-temperedly: 'No, it doesn't bother me, it disgusts me – so change those sheets!' I immediately telephone the young inspector. The cracked clay of the poultice grips like a pillory. My words tumble from my mouth. He tells me: 'There's nothing I can do for you. I've already said this business is out of my hands now. Phone my colleague at Paris headquarters. This is his number.' At the headquarters nobody is in the picture. I tell them my name, that of my aunts, remind them of the date of our statements. Never heard of them. The inspector in charge of the case is away on holiday for a week. I ask to speak to his associate; he's not there; then whoever's willing to listen to me. A placid individual tells me: 'There's nothing we can do for your protection. We're short-staffed. Be careful. Don't open the door to anybody, and if they call again, get your phone-number made ex-directory. At the first sign of trouble, call the emergency services; we'll turn out in a matter of minutes. But don't get unduly alarmed; from what you've told me, I'd be amazed if they telephoned again. It's not in their interest to make things worse for themselves; the lines might be tapped. In my opinion they've only been in contact to know how things stand, to find out whether a complaint has been lodged. That's all that matters to them, now that they have the money.'

*

Oddly enough, what I most fear for is my diary, the red notebook I've taken three years to fill, which bears the trace of evenings spent with Vincent, and whose last page was written a fortnight ago. If it were to disappear, if it were stolen! One day Vincent said to me: 'I'm glad to be making you write, that you're writing thanks to me.' But on another occasion he cast a suspicious glance at the notebook, and he said: 'I hope you're not putting everything down in detail!' I'm having dinner with Mathieu, back this morning from Brazil; I phone T. to tell him I'll be calling by in a taxi to leave my diary with him. He'll take the opportunity to give me a duplicate set of keys. Because of the threats I'll be staying in the room he had when he was a child. When, in the courtyard of his house, I hand him my diary, he tells me, deeply distressed; 'I'm getting your bed ready, but I can't find a little picture of the Island of Swans I was very fond of when I was a small child. You know, I let a boy stay in the room a few weeks ago. And I went out of my way to tell him, when I showed him the picture, that I was enormously attached to it . . .'

*

I didn't go to sleep at T.'s place. Perhaps the vodka I drank in Mathieu's company helped me reach this decision. I've no intention of entering into this cycle of fear. Why should I be more afraid this evening than the previous one, when I knew nothing of the threats, any more than in a fortnight, when I could have forgotten

HERVÉ GUIBERT

them? On the morning of the 28th I decide to get
Hamsun's last book, *On Overgrown Paths*, in which the
old man of eighty-six, repudiated because of his Nazi
sympathies, leaves out of his speech for the defence
everything that might exonerate him . . . In the Jardin
du Luxembourg, where I go to read, the celebration of
the first fine days is under way. The underhand
squabbling for the chairs with arms, and for the
comfortable ones for sunbathing; the school kids, happy
to be lightly dressed, dodging in and out among the
droplets from the fountains, a pleasant way of cooling
off; I encounter very pretty young girls with their
physics homework; old men, a bit round-shouldered, in
dark suits, are doing crosswords or surreptitiously
jotting down arcane notes on little scraps of paper. I feel
close to Hamsun, I like him even in this downfall, in the
insolence of his courage. For a few moments I see the
world through his eyes: it's true that life is splendid. I
remember, from a few years ago, something I'd
forgotten until now. My father had sent me a letter
from the Mediterranean island where he was spending
his holidays. Because of a nasty bout of bronchitis
he could no longer bathe in that sea he loved so much.
So he went for walks and explored the places we had
discovered, he and I, when I was 'his friend'. In his
letter he wrote: 'Those are an old man's memories. But

that's as it should be. I hope you have taken on board a little of that wisdom I have had so much trouble in teaching you.'

*

Hamsun has gone deaf. He is washing himself, naked to the waist in his underpants. He is surprised by a pretty young girl he has not heard knocking on his door and who finds him in this slightly ridiculous situation; to make matters worse, he has not had time to put his false teeth back in. The evening before I left for the country, dropping in uninvited on my great-aunts, for the first time I saw Suzanne lying in bed without her false teeth. She was a different person, an old woman with sunken cheeks, a woman I had never met before. At the same time I was grateful that chance prevented me from being unaware of this truth; isn't it quite something to be aware of a new aspect of those we love, terrible though it might be? Hamsun surreptitiously read the newspapers which had been forbidden him in his old-people's home. He wrote: 'I thus learned, for the first time, of the scandalous acts of the Germans in our country.' The other day I told Louise of the leisure-time activities of the militants of the National Front who, egged on by the rantings at a meeting, had indulged in a cute little coon-hunt in a suburb of Marseilles. I told Louise of the terrified young Arabs who jumped out of windows to escape. Her look made it clear to me that she would be changing her vote.

*

Before leaving for dinner, I write in my diary a sentence dictated by a sudden, unexpected thought: 'One day a young boy will come into my life who will be a trap.' I don't know why I write this. Ordinarily I understand what I write. I believe this sentence refers to some vague future, like a card-reader's prediction; I don't imagine it might apply to anything past.

*

At eight twenty-five in the evening, from the restaurant where, for the second evening running, I'm dining with Mathieu, conscripted to administer urgent first-aid among friends, I call Vincent's telephone number from which, an hour earlier, I'd had no reply. His mother tells me: 'I haven't seen him. He was in and out like a flash just before I got back. But he called to ask me for a telephone-number. He told me he was with a certain Dom-Tom, whoever he or she might be, it must be

Dominique. He's left his address-book here; would you like me to look? The trouble is it's classified by proper names . . . Just a moment . . . I've found the Dominiques . . . Would you like me to give you the three numbers?' I say no, thank my accomplice, hang up. I had decided to take one of the sleeping-pills Mathieu has given me and to leave the phone off the hook so as to have a good night's sleep at last. But, after an hour of anguish, I put it back on; I'd prefer to hear the gangsters rather than believe, wrongly, that they hadn't called me. The sleeping-pill doesn't do anything for me: despite my exhaustion, I don't sleep all night; I've lost the habit of sleep.

*

Wednesday the 29th, at ten past nine, I wake Vincent who has to be at work at nine-thirty. He's not merely vague on the phone, he's inexplicably unpleasant. That makes three days I've been trying to get in touch with him. I've left messages. He hasn't responded. I ask him to give me no more than ten minutes of his time during his lunch-hour, or in the evening before he leaves. I absolutely must speak to him. I appeal to him in the name of friendship. He refuses; out of spite he gives me my marching-orders. I wanted to suggest to him again a

75

week-end by the Atlantic; I have the feeling that it's
getting on for the time when I'll be in crucial need of it.
I was counting on explaining this to him by word of
mouth; this time, whatever happens, we really must
promise to take that trip together. What bothers me
most is to hear a voice that has changed its tone, as if,
behind the behaviour and the personality, there were
those of another person. It reminds me unpleasantly of
the change in the voices of my aunts in the week before
my return. That way of inserting, after each question, a
noticeable break between the thought of the answer
and the answer itself which is more than a prudence – a
symptom.

*

Around ten my great-aunt Louise phones to tell me that
she has just noticed that a further seventeen millions in
savings certificates and Government Stocks, most of
them not registered, have disappeared from the bag in
which she'd hidden them at the back of the cupboard in
her room. She had checked that the bag was still there,
without wishing to handle its contents, convinced that
the man with the white teeth, the daddy of the little boy
with the double hare-lip, was incapable of theft. The
discovery, perhaps her greatest disappointment, even

more than the death-threats that hang over me, raises the total amount extorted to seventy-four million old francs. I have to notify the police. Once again, on the telephone, I am in contact with one of the inspectors working on the case. The suave, bureaucratic voice inclines me to think the police have already shelved the case, that the police-commandos have put on their show as if to outshine that of the gang; everything has lapsed into a state of oblivion and impunity. The gangsters spent a week working on the case, the police a couple of days: other fish to fry. A second 'dactylo' ought to be called in to take the prints of the police and make sure we haven't been dealing with a mirage. It would seem this police force possesses a magic formula with which to cover up its incompetence to sort out the business that one is concerned with: kept busy with another, more urgent case – and how! – 'A rape', the cop excusing himself whispers, with a mysterious, almost lubricious air.

*

I give my father Knut Hamsun's *Pan*. The first thing he asks me, after embracing me, is: 'That brooch, what is it? Saint George?' I've just been telling him about the business with the gangsters. His expression becomes tense when I mention the threats. I continue: 'For a few months now curious things have been happening to me, random incidents which all seem to fit together. I'm put into dangerous situations, but each time something comes to my rescue, as if by a miracle, as if this badge were in fact protecting me. It's a series; one day it surely must be broken. It began in Nîmes, last June, at the end of the Feria. Hans Georg had gone back by train. I was alone with Vincent, who was going out of his way to avoid me, returning at dawn, when he returned at all, and Gottfried, our German friend, who would take the night train to Spain. Gottfried and I were walking among a crowd. We'd left Vincent in a square at a reggae concert. Gottfried said: "Let's go for a walk in the Jardins de La Fontaine. They're so beautiful. We've still got a little time. It'll be quieter." Whoever had suggested that walk to me, I'd have envisaged danger. The very personality of Gottfried excluded the idea; so self-confident, so forceful, so knightly. The gates of the Jardins were closed. I was almost relieved. But Gottfried took me in through the café; once we were past the suspicious glances of the waiters on the point of closing the place, there we were, inside the gardens, quiet, happy, in the mild, blue-tinged warmth of the evening. Little by little we left behind us the chaos of the Feria, making our way to the upper part of the gardens by way of its dense surrounding thickets. "Don't be afraid," said Gottfried, "you're with me." We halted on an esplanade. The sounds were muffled. Down below we could see the lights of the festival glimmering in a halo of firecrackers. How content we were! How silly it had been to be apprehensive! It was a great idea to have come here. We breathed deeply. The air we exhaled seemed to be freeing us from the violence the Feria had accumulated in us for a week – we were still there in appearance, but in reality we were far, far away . . . We started walking again. All of a sudden Gottfried said to me: "I think I'm getting to be like an animal." He has very sharp hearing; he had heard a sound of moving bodies, muffled by the undergrowth we were crossing. Eight shadows, bunched together, were coming towards us. A black dog dashed between us. I thought: we were mad to come here; this could be dangerous; there's nobody about; shouting would be of no use. But no, it was my paranoia. The boys had passed us and, laughing, one of them had called out: "Is that dog chasing you, then?" Gottfried had replied very calmly: "No, it's a very good dog." I thought: just the right thing to say, saves us from any funny business. We went on walking, side by side. Gottfried whispered: "They're following. Don't turn round. We mustn't run." In no time the gang has surrounded us, there are two revolvers pointed at us, a youth is playing with an iron bar, a voice says: "Give us your money!" They're young Arabs. Gottfried and I, without noticing it, find ourselves separated from one another in the midst of this pack. Each of us is already ashamed of his helplessness towards the other, each is already ashamed of the blood he is going to have to wipe from the other's face, or to admit to on his own. I think: I have eight hundred francs in my left-hand trouser pocket, and my credit-card is in my passport in my inside jacket-pocket; within a second I pull out the eight hundred francs and hold them out to the nearest youth; at the same time I say to him – it bursts from my lips without my thinking of it – "Just tell us how we can get out of here." – "Over there," the youth answers, making a vague gesture with his arm. He hops under a lamp-post to see how much he has clutched in his hand. For him it's a lot. He can't stop himself from jumping for joy. Gottfried is on his knees. He drags his fat wallet from the back pocket of his jeans and solemnly hands it to the attacker. He says: "Give me back my papers. I'm a foreigner." He lets out the words separately, in a murmur; the splitting-up, the slowing-down, the sensation of the importance of the declaration is what strikes me. The youth has snatched his wallet from him, extracted the wad of notes, and thrown it back. A voice cries out harshly: "The watches!" In his tragedian's delivery, Gottfried appeals: "Don't take my watch! That was my father's watch, and he's dead." One of the revolvers has just been pointed at my temple. Is it real? Does it fire an asphyxiant gas? A hand knocks the arm holding the weapon away from me and the voice of the youthful owner of the saving hand delivers a counter-order: "Don't take the watches!" Gottfried has invented the magic formula. We begin running flat out; I'm so shit-scared I scale a tall gate, hang in the void from one of its gilded spikes and let myself drop down into a steep lane. We keep on running. The youths have been counting Gottfried's money; there are Deutsch-marks; more than a million's worth; because of the amount they panic; one of them has just shouted: "We'll have to kill them!" In the empty, sloping lane, with no houses on either side, a little coupé is attempting to get out of its line of parked cars, the driver struggling with his steering-wheel. Without either tipping the other off, Gottfried and I, on either side of the car, force a door open and crawl in over the heads and shoulders of the petrified occupants, to find ourselves seated in the back, begging the driver: "Quick! Quick! Get going! Faster! We're being followed! They want to kill us!" Once out of danger, fear begins to surge through you in waves, ever more

81

overpowering. You seek to forget the scene, but it returns again and again, passes and repasses before your eyes and tortures you all the more because, when it happened, we were too much in a state of shock. We decided not to go to the police. It would finish us off to make statements. Let's go and calm down at the hotel. We lie down side by side on the bed, the windows open on to the brightly lit amphitheatre, vibrating with music and fireworks, transformed for this last night into a nightclub. Gottfried huddles against me. He whispers: "You're my brother in danger. I love you . . ." This body, suddenly willing, that I have for years desired in vain, would have almost disgusted me.'

*

I continue with my story. 'There was a young boy I found very attractive. We spent three nights together, the first two fantastic. We talked from eight in the evening to four in the morning. He'd just arrived from the West Indies where he'd spent the first eighteen years of his life on a beach in the company of two bitches, surfing and sailboarding, always solitary, taking the school bus to go to the capital. At the moment of leaving this young boy I knelt at his feet to kiss the fingers – nothing more, nothing less. It amused me to think how, when I was eighteen and he was sixty, the writer R.B. kissed my hands in this way and, one evening, at a bus-stop, asked me to touch my lips to his tired eyelids. I was thirty, but here I was indulging myself with young boys like a man of sixty . . . The third evening, the boy arrived very depressed, talking only of suicide. About two in the morning, no doubt turning on me the aggression he'd wanted to inflict upon himself, he smashes his glass of champagne against the wall and faces me with the broken, knife-sharp stem, saying: "I'm going to slit your throat." He's calm; I am too. It's a moment suspended between us, of an unbelievable serenity and lucidity – like a gunned down plane looping the loop in free-fall: it's not a question of going to meet danger, any more than it's one of defying it either; this boy could very well cut my throat, just as he could equally well do nothing. Neither of us yet knows, and it's almost none of our business. We're back in the hands of our destinies. At this precise moment the telephone rings. I'm never disturbed at night. Nobody has ever played a trick on me since I've had this number. Who could be calling me at this hour? C. is away in the country with the children, so T. is on his own. It could only be he. He knew I was seeing this boy. He mocks my little affairs. He's trying to find out what's going on.

But it's the voice of a boy I don't know, who, noticing the surprise with which I reply, says: "But it was you, wasn't it, who just gave me your number on the *minitel*?" – "No, it wasn't me." – "But you are wanting something, aren't you?" he says. I look at my companion who is still holding the broken glass at me and, as if it were to him I'm saying it, I answer the boy: "No, I don't want anything." I hang up, get to my feet to take the glass from his hands and go to throw it away in the kitchen. When I return, he says: "There are other glasses . . ." There are, right enough. But it's too late; destiny has passed between us without touching either of us; that unexpected phone-call came at the crucial moment to get us both off the hook. A few days later I find out it was Vincent's friend Pierre who played that fortunate trick on me.'

*

I tell my father a third story. 'That other young boy, the one we call The Poet, came to Paris for the February school holiday. We'd already spent a lot of time together in the Midi, where I'd met him, then for the first time in Paris, then on the island of Elba where he came for Christmas. They were pleasant moments. We're not in love; that gives the relationship a quality of lightness, something freer and more collusive. This time, shortly after his arrival, I get a splinter under my thumbnail. There's no getting it out, either with a needle or a pair of tweezers. The Poet soon becomes like another splinter. It's like a container of nitric acid pouring over my face from an eye-dropper. Burning holes. I'll really have to send it flying. Nothing much to fear for the acid; it will flow together like mercury, and, like ivy, it will climb up someone else. We've just dined early at La Coupole. To get back to my place, we take the road that cuts across the Montparnasse cemetery. We walk on opposite sides of the road. The cars are hurtling along between us; we shout out our mutual insults over their hoods. We get to my street; it's silent, deserted. The Poet breaks into one of his celebrated crazy laughs. I've been on the receiving end of so much of that I ought to be inured, but I've shared so much with him that this makes me implode: this time's going to be the last. I take a dash at him and land him a colossal kick. I aim for the bull's-eye; I want to shatter his balls once and for all! Then I grab him by the shoulders, pin him down on the hood of a car and begin banging his head, one blow, then another, then yet another . . .' At this point in my story, my father bursts into tears; he says: 'I'm sorry, I've just re-membered you as a little boy . . . At least you didn't hurt your friend too much?' – 'No. I immediately became aware of this strength I didn't know I had. I sensed it had many degrees, that I could kill this boy, do him a serious injury, or a little injury, it was the latter I opted for. He was bawling "Hit me! Hit me!" He's very strong, thickset, built like a little bull. Suddenly, to free himself from my hold, without warning he throws me backwards, I topple over, lose my balance. One has eyes in the back of one's head: in the course of that movement that causes me to fall over, in that fall, I locate behind me an enormous slab of concrete. Once again it's a moment suspended, out of time. It's happening very quickly but I have the time to work out an equation between the dynamics of my fall, the position of the slab and that of my body which I can no longer control. It's inevitable that my head will smash against that milestone. Then I become calm and I await the big bang. Instead I hear a voice, piping, disincarnate, sexless, like that of a 1940s actor, a saint or a devil, at all events from the beyond, saying: "You mustn't hit each other my children, God loves you, He loves you both . . ." By the looks of it He's also loved my head; I've fallen on my elbow, very close to the milestone. I sit up and see, bending over me, a bearded man, wearing a hat, an evangelist's bag in his hand, who smiling repeats, "You love each other and God loves you, so don't hit each other any more . . ." The Poet is walking away down the road. The angelic little cyclist is in the lapel of my jacket. When I turn round again, the man has mysteriously vanished.' – 'I always knew, and so did your mother, that you'd get yourself murdered,' says my father. 'She consulted a clairvoyant, who predicted it.'

*

In the bus a well-dressed old woman, sweaty, masticates her false teeth. Every now and then she seems to choke on them, as if to vomit them out. If she's doing this, clearly it's to ease some suffering. Little matter the looks people might give her, her mind's made up and the same goes for the embarrassment they might feel, to the point of nausea: more to the point is the lessening of the pain. Behind the woman seated opposite me grinding her teeth, is an attractive young boy. I look at him from time to time and I have the impression that his gaze, which intercepts mine and takes it in, is identical to my own, which understands the old women's mastication.

*

I've just bought myself a pair of nail-scissors. It's

perfectly stupid, but it's an act of bravado. For years an equivocal hesitation holds me back and I cut my nails with scissors all flaky with rust which, the first time I missed would give me a good dose of tetanus – I've never had a booster shot of vaccine. I have the impression of rebelling, by this trivial purchase, against my great-aunts, against the slow paralysis of the stinginess which association with them has enveloped me in like a cape. They wash their hands with lumps like parmesan, useless as soap for decades past; treat their ailments – or infect themselves – with potions and balms from the chemist shop, which their successor refused to buy twenty-five years ago, because they were already beyond their sell-by dates. Avarice begins at home: it's easy to be niggardly with others when one's like that with oneself. That way one's covered. For months I've been hesitating to treat myself to that little picture of a beached ship in an oblong frame. I hang around outside the antique-dealer's shop-window, a poor wretch haunted by his moral heritage. Relieved at having bought the scissors, like a child with its lucky-mascot animal, I've given my angelic little cyclist a great big noisy kiss.

*

For the third evening running Mathieu has the chore of dining with me. For the second evening running I phone Vincent's mother, my informant, from the restaurant. She says: 'But didn't you speak to him this morning?' – 'Yes, but he was so out of sorts he hadn't anything to say.' I ask her to keep this conversation private, between ourselves: 'For six years now I've thought of myself as a friend of Vincent's. You've often sensed my frustration on the telephone, and you've been kind enough to make it easier for me. On one occasion I was foolish enough to confide in Vincent about this, to tell him you were an ally, always ready to keep me posted about his comings and goings. And he made a scene . . . I'm going through a particularly painful and worrying period. I need the support of my friends; and that's where Vincent is letting me down, totally and inexplicably. At least, he's not ill – is he?' – 'I don't think so,' his mother replies, 'but I must say, for my part, that for some days now we've found him extremely odd. He doesn't talk any more. He wanders through the place like a zombie, picks at his food in the dining-room, and goes off again.' I slip in: 'This evening – has he taken his motorbike?' – 'He hasn't got a motorbike,' his mother replies. She tells me the next day she's off on her holidays for ten days with her husband. She has to see Vincent again to sort out with him the arrangements about the car, to see whether or not he'll be needing it. I wish her a pleasant holiday. She says: 'I hope you'll find again with Vincent the warmth that you deserve.'

*

I've decided this evening to sleep at T.'s place, to change, if not my ideas, at least my dreams or nightmares. I telephoned C. in the afternoon to warn her, to ask her to leave keys to the room out for me. She tells me she'll have left for the country with the children. When I arrive at ten o'clock the shutters are closed. I find the house dark and empty. Stupefied, I watch television for a couple of hours. Then I brush my teeth. Towards midnight I go to bed, but not in the room that's been made up for me; I slip into T.'s and C.'s bed. I feel as if I'm the little girl in the story who secretly tries out, one after the other, the chairs and the beds in the house of the big bears and the little bears to see which is the most comfortable, leaving them rumpled behind her. One of the children has left a little rubber tortoise in the bed. Waiting for sleep to come, I press it in my hand; but sleep doesn't come, it still doesn't come. One o'clock, two o'clock . . . T. isn't back. He's dining with that actress who was going to tell him she's leaving him – T. is a theatrical agent. During the day I spoke to him several times on the phone; he's taken my diary to photocopy it and give it back to me. He'd thought of sending it back by courier. I protested: 'You're crazy. That diary's three years of my life. I value it like one of my own hands – the one that doesn't write . . .' T. hasn't returned, and I suddenly think he's lost the diary, that he's searching for it in vain, that he doesn't dare come back. At half past two, there he is back in the room. His actress has indeed left him, but he's calm. It's strange to be back in bed with one's best friend, almost an incest. For the first time T. spits my come out into his hand and goes to wash it away. We only sleep for four hours . . . In the morning T. inspects his sex, says it feels itchy. He adds: 'I must be allergic to your saliva . . .'

*

Last autumn when there was that wave of terrorist attacks in Paris, a couple of days after the most violent – the bomb stuffed with shreds of iron, the better to rip up its victims, the one thrown from a car in the rue de Rennes outside that Tati store – we had an amazing conversation at my friend Bernard's place. The previous evening Bernard had seen an acquaintance of his, close to the people suspected of the attacks. Distraught, this man had told him: 'For months a young student used to

91

come to the house, really charming, very sharp, I like him a lot; yesterday he arrived in a state of indescribable agitation. He begged me to let him sleep at my place – which he'd always refused to do before. In the meantime I'd heard of the attack in the rue de Rennes.' A question was posed among Bernard's guests: what to do in such circumstances? My answer abruptly ended the discussion: 'Me, I'd turn them in on the spot, if I had any proof. Even my best friend. Even T., I'd even be capable of turning him in . . .'

*

The gangsters have changed the way we look at each other, my great-aunts and I, each of us as regards the two others. It's as if all three of us were suddenly seen naked, something like that, worse than that . . . I put Suzanne and Louise on their guard: 'When it comes to the family, don't overdo it with talk about "Louise is mad" or "Suzanne has gone gaga"; we've already seen well-meaning families have their old people put away to speed up the realisation of their assets . . .' – 'This business will have done for me anyway,' Suzanne tells me. 'It's been the finish of me. There are times I'm not sure I haven't dreamt it.' For all that she reckons on taking advantage of some cheap familial labour: 'All those pots of paint left in the garden – you couldn't carry them up into the store-room, could you?' Suzanne, who hasn't lifted anything for fifty years, can't imagine that those pots cannot be moved by someone like myself, let alone by her eighty-one-year-old sister ... The news item of the day – it's only once a week, filtered through my great-aunts, that I catch up with world-events: in Lyon, in the cold-store of a firm that makes ready-to-eat meals, they've found meat that **wasn't** just covered with mould but teeming with maggots. One day Suzanne showed me how much she enjoyed sucking at a rotten fig. She'd just gone purple in the face in a grimace of hatred when I'd told that, the evening before, I'd had a splendid dinner with my father; she'd dearly have loved, if we had to eat, that we'd dined on the mouldy stuff in the news item. She said: 'So you dined at La Coupole, eh? Oh well, nowadays they're bound to be serving frozen food there.' When I come back upstairs, sheepish, from the garden, where I've tried in vain to shift the pots of paint, I catch Suzanne blushing scarlet, caught out in her fibbings; as I enter the apartment I've interrupted Louise who was in the middle of saying: 'I swear to you those pots of paint are very, very heavy . . .' Suzanne thought I wasn't being straight with her. I'll be getting out of their way, otherwise they'll wear me down.

Thanks to my intervention the gangsters haven't been able to do them in; but they in their turn won't let me get off lightly . . .

*

A little girl, that's the first impression Suzanne made on me when I was a child. She wore nasty, hand-me-down shoes that were too small and drew down on her the gibes of the local little brats. For the daughter of a railwayman the depths of suffering lay in social humiliation. Having come up to Paris, become a pharmacist's wife, she slaves away over her accounts book and her till from which, all her life, she sees the money siphoned off: by her husband for his whores, by dishonest employees, by her own hand, putting something aside, by her mother, who asks her to turn a blind eye. The money piles up; apart from some belated package-tours, she never has the pleasure of it: it doesn't belong to her. Her husband, who carries on dreadfully at her, has a well-used leitmotif – 'One can always tear up a will!' When, at his death, the lawyer tells her she's the heir, on condition she sets aside a certain sum for the mistress who bled him dry, she can't get over it. She's become a cripple. She can't travel any more. What'll happen to the money? The whole family is lying in wait. Suzanne and I have lived together fifteen years in an incredible, unexpected friendship, each for the other. For all that, every now and then, a perverse blade seems to be intent upon severing it, burning it away: the electricity of money. A dreadful suspicion that could be the ruination of all hope, and with that of life itself: suppose I were a scoundrel?

*

I've got in touch with Vincent at his work; on the telephone he's once again easy going and warm. I laugh in an embarrassed way at my false alarms. We're leaving together very soon in the car his mother has left for him. I'll be calling in for him when the shop closes. To the Atlantic coast! I go to see my great-aunts for one last time. When I arrive, Suzanne is in the process of dying. She says: 'I was looking at the clock and saying to myself, he'll never see me alive again . . . I love you so much . . . I'm so happy to see you once more.' Her words give me a boost; and she's suffering, she's dying! This isn't the first mini-coronary. She's already had ten, and described them to me in detail. This time I'm there. She presses my hand to her chest, there where the infernal pain is stifling her, ravaging her breathing. Louise prepares the drops, then crushes the tablet. I think she's being very slow about it. I try hard not to get in a panic. I smile at Suzanne, who's ravaged by the stroke. Through the paper wrapping I show her two red buds in the bouquet: 'They're the first peonies, my favourite flowers . . . You like them too, don't you?' My efforts, those of Louise, the medicines, succeed in getting Suzanne back on her feet. As soon as she revives, her tender affection evaporates. She tells me: 'You're going to have to try to go from the balcony to the terrace. The door's jammed. Perhaps you'll manage to open it from the inside.' I try to do as she asks: I'm not agile. I have to get myself across several metres of cornice above a sheer drop. I've no head for heights. I give up. I take a pride in not taking the risk. Suzanne is furious. I've noticed that the pots of paint have been shifted. I ask Louise who did it; she replies: 'I did.' How has she been able to do this, with her sciatica, with her corset? Suzanne is making me forget she's almost died. Everything she says is bitter, selfish, spiteful. For the first time in my life I hate her. She has succeeded in what she set out to do. She has worked hard for it for fifteen years. I've just discovered her secret: the vital need for hatred – to arouse it, to draw it to her like lightning, like love. I hate her; but she's a character of my own creation.

*

Somewhere between Paris and Croix-de-Vie,
the night of the 30th to the 1st.

T.

I'm writing to you because I fear that from now on
everything I might write these days will be taken
away from me. So I'm sending you these letters as I
go along, so that they're in safe keeping. Forgive me
if they're hardly any concern of yours. Circumstances
force me to make use of a mailing address and I've
chosen you as my *poste-restante*. Don't be annoyed.
You are the last person in whom I have confidence. I've
never been so afraid for a manuscript – I have the
impression that it is it, not I, whose life is at risk.
Before leaving I went to photocopy it. I had to hand
over to the shop-assistant every one of its hundred
and twenty-two pages. It was painful, so strange
for me to see all those newly darkened sheets. If
anybody had told me, a fortnight ago, before I got
involved in this business despite myself, that the end
result would be this book, I wouldn't have believed
them. Fortunately I don't consult fortune-tellers. I'd
have gone mad. Perhaps I already have, and this whole
book is the proof of that. I'm the one they're going to

have to lock up. We've driven all night. Vincent has stopped in a lay-by to get a bit of sleep. As my father used to. I'm not sleepy. On the radio they're saying that a mass of cold air has reached us from the North Pole. Apart from that, all they're talking about is the Pope's visit. I'm putting these two sheets, folded in four, in my pocket; before that, much love.

Croix-de-Vie,
1 May

T.

Vincent is sleeping. I don't know if I've ever told you how he sleeps. I know what you're thinking: what a slob! He drops off asleep on his back and his left wrist, adorned with a multicoloured cloth bracelet, is bent limply above his torso, so that his fingers, loosened in an unconscious femininity, suspended as if by magic, barely touch it. I've watched Vincent sleeping when he was still a child. I sometimes suspect I only love him because of this configuration of his when he's asleep, this little picture I paint in my mind and which he'll never be able to see. It came back to me again this morning – the feeling of being here with him only to watch him sleep. But for that, everything else would be a disaster. This trip is a fiasco. At the moment of leaving Paris I had the feeling I was organising my own evacuation. The car was my ambulance. For hours now my nerves have been letting me down. I've felt it, I've felt this nervous exhaustion getting on for madness. Vincent is propelling me headlong into another danger. He smokes. He forces me to smoke. He's brought along a little packet of Congo dope. It's too strong for me. Instead of helping me relax it makes me paranoid. We were stopped at a roadblock and searched. They've increased surveillance because of all the attacks that have preceded the Pope's arrival – you've heard about those bombed churches? With the dope, I was dead scared. But Vincent has the devil's own nerve: he let them body-search him, his hands in the air; with the dope in his fist! I forgot to tell you last night what I did about my manuscript: after photocopying it, I went to the post office and sent the duplicate to myself in a big jiffy bag, registered post with acknowledgement of receipt. I'll go and collect it when I return. Just as I was filling in the form I felt myself caught in a trap: I'd forgotten that one also has to indicate the sender's name. I almost tore up the paper. You know that the addressee can be his own sender, that it wouldn't have made any odds to them? In two minds, I gave Vincent's name as the sender and his address. That was stupid, I should have given yours. It's too late. If anything happens, try to get the packet back from the post office, passing yourself off as me . . . We still haven't gone out. The weather is really filthy. I have the impression that Vincent is going to sleep non-stop for forty-eight hours. I'm going off to post this, along with last night's letter. I was washed out then, I was really out of it. Don't get worked up if I've written you a load of nonsense, take it as it came to me. I haven't the guts to re-read it. Much love.

Croix-de-Vie,
still 1 May

T.

Vincent is still asleep. I've tried to wake him so we can go down to have lunch. Nothing doing. He mutters, he sighs, burrows deeper into the bed; when I keep on at him he gets abusive, threatens me. If he's on drugs

they're keeping him lucid enough to find the most
hurtful words. You can imagine what fun it is to pick
among the innards of a dressed crab, in a dining-room
decorated with fishing-nets and seashells, with sheets
of rain outside the window. When we arrived this
morning it wasn't raining, but everything was horribly
grey. In a little village, shortly before we arrived here,
the wall of a church was spray-painted in red with, in
enormous letters, the words: 'Eat me.' They're writing
all sorts of crazy things like that to protest about the
Pope's visit. Eat me, Vincent, little bad wolf . . .
Upstairs in the room I lay down on the bed beside him,
without venturing the least movement. I thought of my
body, under its clothing, so close to his, naked under
the sheets. With these scars which, so the doctor has
told me, the shingles is going to leave on my abdomen
for at least three years, this body has become a degree
more uninviting; imagine for yourself the state of
elation that puts me in: I'm happy that my thirty-year-
old man's body is seeking by every means to enter into
contact with the corpse it's going to become. It was
high time those two got to know each other better.
Vincent's wrist no longer wants to absent itself from
his torso – it's as if love had cast a spell over it. These
freeze-frames are exasperating; it's no longer a picture,
it's a sculpture! I wriggle about, I sneeze, pull on the

covers to disturb the bed: no go. I toss a sheet over it. It's swallowed up. All of a sudden I've noticed that there's something different in the sounds, in their rhythm, their swings between heaviness and weightlessness; the deluge has mutated into something muffled but also powerful, as if a great wind were dancing outside, paralysing everything it touched. I get up to look out of the window: it's snowing. On the first of May. I'm not dreaming. No need to pinch myself. Those are big snowflakes, swirling and melting into the calm sea, white with the mist rolling off its surface. It's beautiful! I tried to wake Vincent so he could see it. It really is incredible to have snow on the first of May. I thought we ought to take advantage of it to go to Trou du Diable, which would be even more beautiful. But we'd have to be quick, before the snow stopped. Vincent grunts: 'Go fuck yourself!' I went downstairs to the reception-desk to ask about the times of the tides. The landlady, the chambermaid, the cook and the waiter, bunched together behind the door, were watching the snow falling. They were saying it was the Pope's visit that had upset the weather. The landlady said: 'They've burnt another church, it's coming closer. Luckily we're not on his itinerary!' I checked the time of the high tide; there wouldn't have been any point in going to Trou du Diable. There wouldn't have been anything to see except the great sombre building on the other side of the road and, at the very back of the cave, the entrance which, during the war, opened on to a passage leading to its cellars and was walled up . . . I'm in room 17 of the Hotel des Embruns, Boulevard de la Plage, Croix-de-Vie, Vendée, with Vincent, who's still sleeping. It's still snowing. Perhaps the car won't be able to get started again and the little seaside resort, where snow hasn't been planned for, is going to be cut off? I'm fantasising. My manuscript is hidden away in my luggage, wrapped up in a piece of clothing. Vincent is too out of it to nose about there. All the same, I tell myself I've been incredibly careless; if I'm any judge of the way things stand, the book's at his mercy. The receipt for the registered postage of the copy is in my jacket-pocket, in his name and, as soon as I leave the room to post these letters to you, the original is within his reach. If, by chance, for any reason the book were lost, I beg you to tear up the letters. Much love.

Croix-de-Vie,
still 1 May

T.

I haven't told you anything about Croix-de-Vie, about these landscapes I wanted to see again, that I have already seen again in so many dreams, ever since I realised they were haunting me. In these apparitions they were sometimes as they used to be, sometimes destroyed. On one occasion I dreamed of a skyscraper built on the sea-wrack. At each of its hundreds of windows a local woman wearing her white lace coif was beckoning to me . . . The Hotel de la Plage, where we used to stay, has its sky-blue shutters up. It isn't the season. The white cement guardrail I used to trail a hand along hasn't been repainted. The two-tone tents still haven't been set up on the beach, nor have the bathing-huts. The only things left out are the deal boards that contain the movement of the sand at the spring tides and cool one's bare feet from the boiling-hot sand underfoot. All the three waffle-stands are closed: there's no smell of pancake-batter beginning to smoke, nor of jam . . . The crossbeams of the Club des Corsaires are still embedded in the dough of damp sand, which is crumbling away with the burrowing of sand-fleas; the iron is rusting. The low tide has exposed the diving-board, leaving behind alluvial deposits, sluggish rivulets that trickle from the mud, pending the arrival of the children's sandcastles. How marvellous it was to dam them, to divert them and to construct networks of lakes into which they flowed, barrages strengthened with pebbles to head them off. You could spend hours watching the meagre streams of water dribbling over the surface of the sand. Time stood still. On the glittering edge of the outgoing tide rose-pink starfish by the dozen lie on their backs dying. To the right of the beach, where the waves break at high tide, there rears up the rock they call La Grenouille. Further off, at the turn of the bay – what an overwhelming mass of rock it is! – the silhouette of a bear of a man, carrying a child on his shoulders, stands out against the light. Only it's a bit smaller than it used to be. Everything has shrunk. The rediscovered landscape has become a scale-model of the landscape of childhood. No trace of a kite on the horizon. The brown expanse of slippery seaweed still awaits me, with my rubber sandals, my white Breton-style cap, my red bucket and my shrimping-net which I've forgotten to wash out in fresh water; it stinks pleasantly of shrimp. I'll prod about in every inlet until it yields up to me the giant crab that will nip me till the blood comes. I go on still further, at the risk of being cut off by the rushing, incoming tide; if I manage to go on walking another five minutes, I'll reach the Trou du Diable by the ford . . . Vincent is still asleep. At times he stops breathing. I wonder if he's dead. I wonder if he'll be getting up for dinner. The snow has stopped falling, but I haven't stopped loving you.

*

High tide will be at 11.57 a.m. I wake Vincent. He's slept without a break for more than twenty-four hours. He must be exhausted, that's all I can say. Why would he believe the business about the snow? He'd only have had to ask the first passer-by and he'd have known it was true. But he's not interested. He's just rolled a joint. In a foul mood, he tells me: 'Cool it with your raptures! Your Trou du Diable, your fucked-up plans, they get on my nerves. If you go on like that, I'll headbutt you, I'll do for you . . .' He's refused to go to the Trou du Diable on foot. He says he's tired. We take the car, follow the coast beyond the beach, take the first turning, the second, then drive straight on. From my side I watch out for the building behind its lime trees. I'm afraid it might have been demolished. 'Stop,' I say to Vincent, 'it must be over there.' There are no tourist coaches or family cars. There's nobody about. The weather's so vile. I run down a little sloping path. The sea is hidden from me by the bushes. From far behind Vincent is following me. I hear the breathing of the chasm, its call. I remember the well of black, sharp-edged rock, the way it has of streaming out, far from itself, of decanting itself, of emptying itself before, groaning, it boils up again and gushes forth. There's a coping above the chasm; I'd forgotten that. I wait for the sea to be sucked out by the receding wave before stepping forward. I walk, keeping my balance. I take care. It's a pleasure to defy my vertigo. Perhaps after this I won't feel it any more; it's so unnerving – at the least unevenness, the slightest gap . . . I'm in the process of curing myself. I only have to get to the far side of the chasm. I haven't heard him coming. I feel Vincent's hands at my back. Are they pushing me or are they stroking me?

Marks of Identity
Juan Goytisolo

Marks of Identity is the first volume of Goytisolo's major trilogy. The other two books, *Count Julian* and *Juan the Landless*, and Goytisolo's most recent novel, *The Virtues of the Solitary Bird*, are also published by Serpent's Tail.

'For me *Marks of Identity* was my first novel. It was forbidden publication in Spain. For twelve years after that everything I wrote was forbidden in Spain. So I realized that my decision to attack the Spanish language through its culture was correct. But what was most important for me was that I no longer exercised censorship on myself, I was a free writer. This search for and conquest of freedom was the most important thing to me.'

Juan Goytisolo, in an interview with *City Limits*

'Juan Goytisolo is by some distance the most important living novelist from Spain . . . and *Marks of Identity* is undoubtedly his most important novel, some would say the most significant work by a Spanish writer since 1939, a truly historic milestone.' *The Guardian*

'A masterpiece which should whet the appetites of British readers for the rest of the trilogy.'
Times Literary Supplement

'It is a good thing Goytisolo is finally being published in America; we need his pages, open as they are to the flutesong of sex and the polyphony of diverse culture.' Edmund White in the *VLS*

Also published by Serpent's Tail

The Lonely Hearts Club
Raul Nuñez